Friend of the Court

A Joth Proctor Fixer Mystery

Books by James V. Irving

Joth Proctor Fixer *series*
Friends Like These
Friend of a Friend
Friend of the Court

Coming Soon!
Friend of the Devil

Friend of the Court

A Joth Proctor Fixer Mystery

James V. Irving

SPEAKING VOLUMES, LLC
NAPLES, FLORIDA
2022

Friend of the Court

ISBN 978-1-64540-644-0

For Lindsay,
who has yet to give her parents a bad day.

Acknowledgments

Thanks to my agent and wise counsel Nancy Rosenfeld; to Kurt and Erica Mueller at Speaking Volumes, who provided a steady hand at the tiller; and to the creative, energetic voice of my editor, David Tabatsky.

Colleagues and friends Scott Dondershine, Steve Moriarty and Tamar Abrams provided insight and practical advice that I couldn't have done without.

Thanks to Ken Willner, my buddy on F Dock.

I'd be remiss not to acknowledge Gordon R. Butler and M. Morgan Cherry, my former employers at Legal Investigations, Inc., where real life adventure was frequently stranger than fiction.

Thanks to my old roommate Joth Davis who graciously allowed me to borrow his name for use in this series.

A tip of the baseball cap to three jamokes who always seem to be around when I need them: Kevin Kearney, Peter Franklin and Paul Commito.

Particular thanks to my wife Cindy without whom none of this would have been possible.

Chapter One

Down the Rabbit Hole

A week passed before anyone noticed Track Racker's disappearance. I heard about it from Heather Burke when she called my office one dry June afternoon. She skipped our usual pleasantries and cut right to the chase.

"What do you know about Frank Racker?"

The edge in her voice raised my blood pressure. I took that as a warning to tread carefully. Heather was my friend, and had been more than that, once upon a time; but she was also Arlington County's chief prosecutor, and it wasn't always easy to know which hat she was wearing.

"Track Racker? I haven't seen him since our case ended. Why?"

"His wife filed a missing person report."

She sounded curt, even surly, which told me to remain on guard. I knew this call would come one day, but Heather's words were still chilling. Through all the ups and downs and bumps and bruises, our baseline friendship had remained secure, but now I felt like this paradigm may have changed, possibly forever.

"Jennifer Carter?" I asked. "You mean his girlfriend? His client's widow?"

"Maybe that explains why she took so long to follow up, but it doesn't explain what happened to him."

"He's probably in Vegas," I said, "spending the insurance money I collected for him."

"I'm going to ask you one more time. Do you know anything about what happened to him?"

"Track lived in Old Town," I said. "Isn't that outside your jurisdiction?"

" 'Lived?' "

As soon as I said it, I wished I could have sucked that last consonant back into my throat. Heather waited and I ground my teeth, reminding myself to avoid any use of the past tense.

"I heard he moved in with her. I don't know if that's true, and if it is, I don't know if that's in Fairfax or Alexandria, but it sure as hell isn't Arlington."

"Heard from who?" she said.

"Don't you have some real work to do?"

I could hear her tapping the eraser end of a pencil on her desk, which only made me want the phone call to end before I said anything else that could raise suspicion.

"Joth, you're not telling me everything."

"I never tell you everything, Heather. You're the Commonwealth's Attorney, for Christ's sake. For all I know, you're investigating my client."

"Is Racker still your client?"

"He will be if you're investigating him."

She paused, waiting for me to rise to the bait, but I refused. I knew her too well, but this was no longer a sport we sometimes played.

"I want to know about this," she said.

"This?"

"You know what I'm talking about."

Through all our personal and professional challenges, the final spark had never been fully extinguished. I was less sad than bitter.

"You'll be on the top of my list," I said. "Promise."

Heather's call rattled me, but it also served an important purpose by alerting me to the existence of an Alexandria police investigation, which was sure to include me in its sweep.

Two days later, I was prepared when a pair of detectives stopped by unannounced. I ushered them to my tiny, untidy office as if it were just another day.

Detective Chester Anderson was a bullish man with a buzz cut. He was dressed in a blue blazer, khakis, and a rep tie—the uniform of the patrician Virginia caste, which his brusque demeanor and overbearing style disqualified him from. I disliked him immediately. I didn't mind social climbers, or even those who traded on the questionable fortune of a society birth. But what annoys me is when people try to pass themselves off as something they aren't.

Fortunately, my instinct for self-preservation overcame my impatience.

Detective Michael McCarthy was a small, chipper man, dressed in a well-pressed light-weight suit. He had a ruddy complexion, which lit up amiably as he showed me his ID and introduced himself and his partner.

"I go by Mickey," he said. "Call me Mickey."

I nodded. I did not intend to get on familiar terms with him. Meanwhile, Anderson took the opportunity to scan every flat surface within the range of his glance.

"What about this guy?" I said, nodding toward Anderson. "Has he got a badge or is he just a trainee?"

With a well-practiced glare, Anderson pulled out his credentials, flashed them at me, and then slapped them shut, as if he wanted me to know that my face could be next. I smiled. I instantly understood two things: I wasn't supposed to like this guy and they thought I was important enough to set up a good cop-bad cop routine in advance. I had no choice but to play along, hoping they'd fall into their own game.

"What can I do for you Detective McCarthy?"

He produced a pocket notebook with a flourish and consulted it.

"This Frank 'Track' Racker. He's a client of yours?"

"As far as I know. I haven't seen him since our case ended."

"What kind of case was that?" said McCarthy.

"A regulatory matter. I'm not going to get into the details of it."

I turned to face Anderson, who was pawing at a pile of documents strewn across the top of my credenza.

"And you get your hands off the paperwork," I said, "or we can step out into the lobby."

Anderson gave me an appraising look, but it was not my imposing size that put teeth into this threat. He knew better than to snoop around a lawyer's documents—at least when that lawyer was in a position to raise a squall about it. But I didn't really care. As far as I was concerned, any tidbit they discovered would have value to me if it distracted them from their purpose.

"Can we sit?" McCarthy said.

"I don't think I've got much to say to either of you."

"Why not?" said Anderson.

"Because I don't like your manners."

McCarthy sighed.

"Look, a guy's gone missing and we're just trying to find him."

"Friend of yours, too, as I understand it," Anderson said.

"Friend of a friend," I said. "A client."

"Any reason you wouldn't want him to turn up?"

I gestured them toward the two captain's chairs bearing the University of Virginia seal across from my cluttered desk. I sat in the well-worn leather chair behind it. Anderson took the opportunity to study my wall hangings, but I knew he'd gain little there. Two framed diplomas and a bar license dominated the wall across from my desk. Above the credenza was a grim pen and ink drawing of the House of the Seven Gables, matted in dark red and framed in somber black. Next to the window was a framed professional photograph of Marblehead Light, a spare lattice work of steel girders shaped like an hourglass and surmounted by the revolving light that had kept lost, inattentive, and careless mariners off the rocky outcropping of Marblehead Neck for centuries.

"Now, about Racker?" McCarthy said.

"We knew each other from lacrosse at UVA," I said.

"Former teammates?"

"No. We didn't overlap, but the lacrosse world is a small community and I stayed involved after I graduated. We lost track of each other over the years. I'd see him every once in a while at an alumni event, but I didn't have any real contact with him until he showed up a couple of months ago, looking for some legal help."

"And you helped him?" McCarthy said.

"Yes, I did. I'm sure he'd tell you that himself."

"He pay his bill?" said Anderson.

I smirked.

Did they secretly know Track?

"That's none of your business," I said, "but the answer is yes."

Anderson got up and began prowling the office. He wasn't really snooping; he was trying to get me off my game.

"When's the last time you saw him?" McCarthy said.

"I think it was the day we settled up. Yeah, I'm sure it was."

"When was that?"

"I'd have to look at my calendar, but sometime in late May. When was Track last seen?"

McCarthy licked the tip of his pencil and jotted something in his notebook.

"That would be May 24th."

"Where was that?"

"At a white nationalist rally in Old Town Alexandria."

I considered the tone of my responses so far and what knowledge I might be expected to have before responding to this intentional provocation.

"Isn't May 24th Confederate Memorial Day?"

"That's right," Anderson said.

"You'd better be careful who you're talking to when you come up with something like that," I said. "A lot of the citizens of the Commonwealth might say that those people were celebrating southern cultural heritage. Track's a reenactor. He shows up with a group of guys periodically to dress up and refight Civil War battles. It seems kind of strange to me, but that's what he told me."

"Confederate sympathizer, too?" McCarthy said.

I knew that Track had little sympathy for anything or anyone other than Track, but I didn't tell them that.

"If he was, I never saw any signs of it," I said. "Like I said, weird, but pretty harmless."

"Did you discuss it?" said Anderson.

"I was born and raised in Massachusetts," I said. "Track knows where I stand on things. He wasn't dumb enough to keep bringing it up."

McCarthy thought for a moment and looked at Anderson, who just glared.

"Does he have any relatives or friends he might be visiting?"

"Not that I know of. He wasn't the sort of guy who made a lot of friends and if he had any relatives, he didn't talk about them."

I glanced at my wall calendar. June was dwindling and the steamy days of summer would soon be upon us.

"If I were a betting man, I'd guess he'll turn up at the Gettysburg reenactment, which must be coming up at the beginning of July."

Anderson spoke up again.

"There's some talk that you think he might have been involved with what happened to your girlfriend, Miss Jennifer Tedesco, a topless dancer."

He mentioned her work, as if I didn't know, like he wanted to twist the knife all over again. Then he consulted a notebook before adding another nugget for effect.

"She worked at a bar called Riding Time."

"She was a nursing student," I said.

Jenny had been accidentally poisoned with arsenic, which had been intended for someone else. That was my assessment, at least, but not everyone agreed.

"Alright," McCarthy said. "Do you know what happened to her?"

"I know she's dead."

"I heard it was suicide," said Anderson. "Any truth to that?"

They were poking at me, the two of them, trying to work a real squeeze. At this point, they'd expect a show of temper, and I gave it to them, at least enough to match their expectation.

"I don't know what happened to Jenny, but I know she didn't poison herself."

"How do you know that?" Anderson said.

"I think this interview's about over."

I stood up and crossed my arms. McCarthy pondered the change in my attitude as he stroked his upper lip with an index finger.

"Anything else you can tell us?" he said.

"I hope Track turns up," I said. "And I'm sure he will."

I reverted to a casual tone as they got up. I walked them to the outside door in the reception area. That's when it occurred to me that while Anderson's questions were intended to test my balance, nothing either of them had asked had been especially probing. Nothing new had been pressed; nothing unearthed, nothing said that could raise any real suspicion. I also realized that this was just a preliminary visit, designed to get a feel for me and my story.

We exchanged cordial goodbyes and handshakes at the door. As I watched them cross the parking lot, I

realized they'd be back, or two others in blue uniforms
might come next time to read me my rights.

Chapter Two

Weathering the Storm

Once they were out of sight, I smiled at Marie, my part-time receptionist, secretary and general stabilizing force who had arrived during the interview.

"Care to guess?"

"I've been working for you long enough to know cops when I see them; cops in a bad mood."

"Cops are always in a bad mood. At least they are when I see them."

Marie was a couple decades older than me, an early retiree looking for extra income and a small level of excitement. She got a bit of both from me and reciprocated by focusing a sharp eye and an attentive ear on all office visitors. She took a keen interest in the diverse characters that came and went and while she wasn't one to venture an opinion unless asked, her perspective was invaluable.

"That's because they know to be careful with you, Joth."

"Yeah, but I've got to remember to be careful with them."

I went back into my office and shut the door. It was ten-thirty in the morning, and I had a full day ahead of me with little to do. As I sat down, I realized the armpits of my shirt were soaked with sweat and my hands were trembling. Had the two cops noticed? And if so, what had they concluded? I sometimes kept a pint of rum in the top desk drawer, more as an affectation than anything else, though I occasionally made myself a drink after five p.m.

I pulled open the drawer, poured a shot into a water glass and downed it, realizing as I did that in all my years of practicing law, I had never done anything like that. Then again, I'd never rolled a dead body over the side of a boat before, either.

The summer sun glared through my window.

"What did they want?"

The familiar voice came from my landlord, DP Tran, an agile, jockey-sized Vietnamese immigrant who had come to this country as a boy. He stepped inside my office, uninvited, as he usually did. DP always moved like a cat, and he was as perceptive as a cat's whiskers, a quality that served him well in the private detective business—or would if he ever got his license restored. I slid the pint back into the drawer, hoping he hadn't noticed.

DP was the only person with enough information to surmise the truth about what had happened to Track Racker, yet he offered no comments, no questions, and he hadn't judged me. "So, what did they want?"

"Trouble."

"Fucking cops."

He plopped into the seat Anderson had vacated.

"They're just doing their job," I said.

I hadn't been sleeping and I'm sure I looked like it. DP looked me over, then changed his posture and leaned forward with his hands folded between his knees.

"What do you say we go down to Riding Time? Have a couple of beers; see if Dan's got any new girls."

This was a surprising suggestion coming from a man as prudish as DP. He read my face and let the thought trail off. That universe seemed far away right now.

"You go," I said. "Say hi to Irish Dan for me."

"The Nats are home tonight. Max is pitching. I could get us a couple of good seats."

"Not tonight."

DP was a wiry man, surprisingly strong in the hands and arms and quick as a puma. He was also a man with nerves equal to any challenge I'd seen him face, a man who could coolly pick a seven-pin cylinder padlock with the assurance of a mother changing her baby's pacifier. This combination of traits made him valuable for any

14

lawyer. He took chances from time to time, and while that made him a little bit dangerous, he knew how to balance risk with reward.

He stood up like a dancer, transferring his weight smoothly without any wasted effort.

"You've done a lot for me," he said. "You've bent the rules to give me work when you can. I'm not a guy to forget that sort of thing. You let me know when I can help. Okay? You just tell me what I can do."

I wasn't quite ready for a new confidant, but whenever I was, I knew I'd want to have a guy on my side with the skills and instincts that DP brought to the game.

"The time may come," I said. "It definitely may come."

He raised a hand.

"It will," he said. "And I'll be there when you need me."

After DP left my office, I sat at my desk, took another shot and waited for the next shoe to drop.

***

Days passed and nothing happened. With no further contact from the police, the silence felt claustrophobic. I didn't hear from Heather either. I wasn't dumb enough to call her, or drop by her office, which is what I habitually did when feeling down or faced with a new challenge. She had been my lighthouse, always available, even when I knew she didn't have the time. Although our romance has been dead for years, she had continued to fill the role of trusted confidant usually occupied by a spouse.

The chill of our recent phone call still felt like the setting of the January sun. All dead and gone, but in reality, it had been that way for years. Or so I told myself.

I considered taking a short vacation up to the Massachusetts coast to get away from the brutal DC heat. I could hike familiar paths along rocky shorelines, get a little sailing in and fill my lungs with clean New England air. But a trip like that would only be an excuse, and I would struggle to explain it when I returned. My absence would fuel suspicions that already seemed to be percolating in certain prosecutorial minds. It would only be a delay in the reckoning I knew was coming. I'd come back to the same unanswered questions: where was Track Racker? What happened to him? And who killed Jenny Tedesco? There was no chance for any relief from that right now. I had to stay and weather the storm, however slow-moving and powerful it might eventually become.

In search of a diversion, I called Melanie Freeman. Now in her early 40s, Melanie still carried herself like the vivacious young lady she must have been not so long ago. She was frank and unpretentious and retained the hallmarks of a faded glamour I found hard to resist— flawless features, a flashing, dimpled smile, and shoulder-length, platinum-colored hair with a beguiling wave. She carried herself with an elegant, confident posture and time had not dimmed the allure of her suggestive curves.

And she may have felt that she owed me. Not only did I get Heather to drop an embezzlement charge against her, I had also found Melanie a job that helped restart her life. Soon after, in the aftermath of Jenny's death and Track's disappearance, I'd begun seeing her. So far, this had only amounted to a few casual dates, like dinner or a movie.

My attention was sporadic and superficial, and she was cautious with me, treating me as a wounded warrior and a potentially redeemable savage project. Perhaps Melanie saw in me her own battles with the bottle, her long stints of loneliness, and a growing professional disappointment.

Melanie worked at an assisted living facility in Del Ray, where her usual shift ended at four. I called her there around three-thirty, hoping to catch her at the right time.

"Haven't seen you in a while," I said. "Got time for dinner tonight?"

"Joth, have you been drinking?"

I was surprised my voice gave anything away, but I'd had enough to feel undismayed and unabashed.

"A pop at lunch," I said.

I hoped it sounded like careless flair.

"Joth, I know the signs. I've lived with them. Don't go down this road."

"That's why I'm calling you," I said. "The Nats are home tonight."

Silence.

"Come on, Mel."

"Don't call me Mel. You need some help, Joth."

"Dinner would be a good start."

"A better start would be for you to go back to church. You won't get all the answers there, but you'll get some, and no matter how bad it gets, they won't turn you away. There's a novena tonight. Why don't you go by with me? How can it hurt?"

"Like hell. That's how it can hurt. Father John ought to focus on saving his own soul as far as I'm concerned. That ought to be a fulltime job."

"That's not fair, Joth."

"John's got nothing I want. And if he ever does, I'll let you know."

"Joth, are you in some kind of trouble?"

"Maybe."

"Do you want to tell me about it?"

She was a mother hen at heart, and for a moment I felt I could trust her.

"I'm alright."

"You're not."

She paused, but I didn't hang up.

"I'll tell you what: when you've gone three days without a drink, call me and we'll talk about it. You know where to find me. Alright?"

"Maybe."

I said good-bye and hung up.

I didn't need to be saved and I couldn't risk being helped. What I needed was a case with some teeth to it, and it came the next day from an unlikely source—Liz Hillman, a domestic relations lawyer with a reasonable grudge against me.

Chapter Three

I, Alone, Can Fix It

Back when I was carefree and still young enough to have girlfriends, I had dated Liz Hillman until I dropped her like a hot rock when Heather came on the scene.

At a time when Arlington, Virginia was still a sleepy, bedroom community populated by federal employees who came and went with each new administration, we were part of a circle of up-and-coming professionals determined to change that. Among our group were future prosecutors and politicians, real estate developers, bankers and even future felons.

Couples came and went in those heady times, but Liz expected more from me. She certainly didn't expect to be unceremoniously dumped for a cute assistant Commonwealth's Attorney. In the long run, it was easier for Liz than it was for me. As a domestic relations lawyer, she had minimal contact with Heather or me. After Heather dumped me, I had to see her in the courtroom, day after bitter day.

Over the years, Liz's hard feelings receded, and I passed her any divorce inquires that came my way. She always expressed cordial appreciation, and reciprocated periodically, though usually with an acid observation about my continuing bachelorhood.

"How are you, Joth?" she said.

She didn't need to identify herself over the phone. She'd been a heavy smoker since before we'd met, and her voice had a throaty rasp that had worsened over the years. I still cared for her enough to be concerned.

"I'm fine, Liz. It's great to hear from you."

"Is it? Well, I like to think so."

Like me, she had never married. Unlike me, she had a thriving practice, a longtime law partner, and a vibrant social life. She cleared her throat to fill the dead spot in the conversation. "I think I've got something for you. It's a little messy."

"Naturally. I can't remember the last time you sent me anything that didn't have a little hair on it."

"That's what you do, Joth, isn't it? Aren't you the fixer?"

"Okay, what's this one all about?"

"Well, first of all, it's kind of a divorce case."

"Divorce case! You know I don't touch that stuff."

"Jesus Christ, Joth, will you shut up and listen?"

That was one of the things I always admired about Liz: she liked to get right to the point, and she had no patience for distractions. As a lawyer who was often sifting through barely relevant what ifs, she tended to keep my eye on the ball.

"Okay, let's hear it."

"The client's name is Rachel Justice, but she goes by Bobbitt."

"Bobbitt?"

"Yeah, I'll bet you had a girl named Bobbitt at that ritzy boarding school you went to."

When we were dating, Liz took public delight in my pedigree. After the breakup, she spoke of it as a badge of shame, as if one of my ancestors had been hung as a horse thief. In fact, the first Jonathan Proctor's clipper ships pioneered American trade in Asian markets, which was really the same thing, only on a grander scale.

"So, no, but I've known women with quirkier names, even down here."

Liz sniffed and continued.

"Bobbitt's husband is Tarry Justice. He's one of the founders of Prestige Bank. Do you know it?"

"Yeah, I've heard of it. A couple of alums of one of the big banks started it a few years ago."

"That's right; a pair of William and Mary grads. And it sounds like they're off to a great start. They've already got nearly half a billion in deposits."

She coughed and continued.

"Here's the wrinkle. Tarry Justice hasn't been seen since he fell off a boat into the Potomac River on New Year's Day."

"Boat?" I asked. "What boat?"

I didn't want to be associated with anyone who'd disappeared from a boat.

"One of those little power cruisers that you see rafted up off Georgetown every summer afternoon."

"He's dead?"

I heard the snap of a cigarette lighter and the sound of her taking a long drag. I took a breath.

"He's not dead. Not as far as anyone knows."

"The body didn't turn up?"

"Nope."

That was a lot to think about. The bottom of the Potomac was getting crowded. I liked the fact that bodies seemed to stay there.

"What's Justice doing on a boat on New Year's Day?"

"That's the first question I asked. Seems he and his business partner—Nick Grimes is his name—had a long-standing tradition of starting the new year with a cruise up the Potomac. Every year, come hell or high water, so to speak. This one didn't end well."

"What happened?"

23

"Well, as I get the story, they had a rather liquid lunch at a bar on the Georgetown waterfront. It was getting dark by the time they left, and they were in a hurry. When Grimes looked back, Justice was gone."

"Life jacket?"

"Of course not."

"Have you talked to Grimes?"

"No, but that's the story. The police were all over it at the time. You probably read about it in the *Post*."

The story rang a bell.

"Doesn't that make Bobbitt a widow?"

"Not without a body. And it doesn't make her a divorcee either."

I thought about how the pieces might fit together.

"What about Grimes?"

"What about him?"

"Did he have any interest in Bobbitt?"

"Why?"

"It would fit a pattern. He'd end up with the bank."

"You know something, Joth? You're a conspiracy monger."

"Is that a yes?"

"It's a firm no. As far as I know."

"Yeah? How far is that?"

"How far are you willing to go?"

I wasn't sure Liz meant it as a joke, but I hoped she had, and I laughed to disarm any ulterior suggestion.

"This isn't about Grimes offing his partner."

"Are you sure?"

"Listen, Joth, nobody thinks that. Grimes and Justice weren't exactly friends, but they'd been together since college, and they were building a booming business together. But let's talk about Bobbitt. She's stuck in legal limbo. Justice is dead and he's not coming back, but the law doesn't care. What are her options? The absence of the husband makes divorce on traditional grounds procedurally tricky. Since he disappeared, it's not like a process server can serve him with a Complaint. There's no obvious way to gain jurisdiction that might not be successfully challenged in the Court of Appeals. It could be years before we get a final ruling that can stick. But Bobbitt knows that she can get immediate access to insurance and testamentary benefits and get on with her life *if* Justice can be declared legally dead."

"I thought you had to be missing for seven years to be declared dead in this state?"

"I'm glad to see you're paying attention. That's the general rule, but there's a rarely used statute that creates an exception. Let me read it to you."

She cleared her throat and cited a section of the Virginia Code, then read from the book that was apparently lying open on her desk in front of her.

" 'Any person on board any ship or vessel underway on the high seas who disappears from such ship or vessel . . .' "

She shut the book and summarized the rest in a sing-song voice.

"Point is, a person can be declared dead six months after the disappearance."

I glanced at the calendar on the wall behind my desk. The first of July would be six months, but that was still more than a week away.

"She's not wasting any time, is she?"

"Can you blame her?"

I pulled up the statute on my desktop PC and studied it.

"Since when is falling into the Potomac 'lost at sea?' "

"Right. That's where you come in, Joth. You're an expert in odd and difficult cases. If anybody can make that argument stick, you can."

There were a few people in the community who thought I might already know too much about people disappearing, but I trusted Liz, and this sounded like a legitimate referral.

"How'd you know about the lost-at-sea statute?"

"I think Bobbitt mentioned it."

"She brought it to your attention?"

"Yup. She said a friend mentioned it to her."

A friend?

I wondered if that friend might be Nick Grimes and I made a mental note to find out.

"She got any money?"

"She will have if you get her husband declared dead."

"I mean now."

Liz paused and took a drag.

"I'm not sure. I know she owns the Major Pelham Inn out in Aldie. You know it?"

"Yeah."

The Pelham was a well-known romantic getaway out in fox hunting country. I recalled it as intimate and cozy, furnished in brass and dark wood, painted in reds and deep greens and featuring stone fireplaces and English hunting prints. But it was small and probably costly to operate.

"I wouldn't think of it as a big money maker."

I sensed a shrug.

"You never know. She looks like she has money."

Liz knew that this didn't prove anything, but her answer suggested that I conflated appearance with reality and this notion offended me.

"What does that mean?"

In fact, it probably meant I'd have a hard time getting paid and that she didn't want me getting cold feet and throwing the case back on her.

"Bobbitt dresses to a T and hangs with the monied set."

"You must know how the Pelham does?"

"Breaks even from what she told me. Puts her in good with the horsey set though. The Middleburg Hunt meets there for breakfast a couple of times a year before they ride to the hounds."

"Is Bobbitt part of that?"

"Aspirationaly. It's hard to imagine her on horse-back."

"Although it's easy to imagine her clinking cocktail glasses in the lounge?"

"Sounds like you've been there."

"Once."

She huffed.

"You never took me there."

"It was a client thing," I said.

But it wasn't. I'd taken Heather there not long after I'd broken up with Liz. While it didn't strike me as the sort of place that made a lot of money, that wasn't my immediate motivation. I needed something to sink my teeth into.

"What's the next step?"

She read off a phone number, ready to end our exchange.

"She's waiting for your call."

Chapter Four

Bobbitt

Bobbitt Justice came in on a Tuesday morning dressed for a Sunday afternoon soiree. Her ash blonde hair bore unmistakable evidence of a recent trip to the beauty parlor. She occupied a chair across from my desk as she assessed my modest quarters with a look of barely concealed disdain, toeing curiously at the pattern on the oriental rug that once decorated a Salem sea captain's parlor. She gave the impression of one not used to dealing personally with the hired help, which is how she apparently regarded me.

Her clear skin and even features made her attractive in a conventional sort of way. Her best feature was a cupid bow's mouth that set her even and extremely white smile to advantage. She knew this and used her varied smiles, pouts, and frowns with the skill of an actress.

Bobbitt appeared to be in her mid-forties and her ample hips strained the seams of a white tennis skirt trimmed in lime green. Middle age had crept up and she seemed to be denying its arrival by refusing to adapt her wardrobe to accommodate the inevitabilities of nature.

She reminded me of the mother of several friends from my youth, women who circulated freely at the chowders and cocktail parties while their spouses competed in regattas.

I watched her eyes focus on my House of the Seven Gables print.

"Are you from up there?"

"I'm from Salem, yes."

"A fan of Hawthorne?"

"He's sort of required reading where I grew up."

"I suppose your people came over on the Mayflower?"

"My 'people?' No. My people came over on the Arbella."

She sniffed dismissively as she turned toward the subject at hand.

"I understand you're the man who tries cases like this."

She smiled, but it held no warmth. She knew this wouldn't be a pleasant meeting.

"There are no cases like this, Mrs. Justice, and no one's tried this one before, at least not in Virginia."

"Bobbitt. Everyone calls me Bobbitt," she said.

Her chilly formality belied the familiarity her name suggested.

"Childhood nickname?"

"No. Tarry made me take his name when we got married. It's in the contact we signed. I think he expected us to have kids. Anyway, I didn't want to be Rachel Justice, I mean, can you imagine? I'd have been the poster child for left wing causes. You know, *Racial* Justice? So, I became Bobbitt."

I filed the political observation away and moved on.

"An old friend's name, I'm guessing?"

"No. After Lorena Bobbitt."

She took a close look at me to see if I recalled the name.

"Just a joke between Tarry and me."

Some joke.

I remembered that Lorena Bobbitt was the Virginia woman who had sliced off her husband's penis with an eight-inch carving knife. That's the kind of detail that tends to lodge in a man's memory. His wife taking his last name must have been awfully important to Tarry Justice.

I could see that Bobbitt was going to be a problem client: imperious, insistent and hard to please, but I never gave a thought to turning the case down. In fact, I found her compelling. I felt like I'd met her before; not Bobbitt Justice herself, but women in her mold—those middle-aged yacht club thrill seekers who were the mothers of childhood friends. These weren't necessarily people I liked or respected, but they tended to have deep stories and artfully crafted facades replacing who they were with who they wanted you to think they were. Instead of feeling repulsed, I was intrigued.

"Okay, Bobbitt."

At first, her green eyes had seemed to be avoiding mine, but now they latched on to me and I saw something else. She had been observing my office and was now studying me as much as I was her—absorbing, looking for telling details. She took in my still-sturdy frame like a fight manager evaluating how many rounds her boxer still had in him. Then she settled on my face— angular with a lot of hard miles, with graying hair in need of a cut. She seemed satisfied by what she saw.

"Well, Liz says you're the man for it."

"Tell me what happened to your husband."

She fingered her pearl necklace.

"Please, Mr. Proctor. I'm sure Liz told you all about it. This is difficult for me."

I'd just met her, but the insincerity tolled like a cracked bell. She sounded like someone who was being careful not to tell her story so many times that the details changed.

"Bobbitt, you need to understand from the start that this isn't going to be easy. If I'm going to fend off problems, I need to know everything."

She looked at me doubtfully and her face twisted into the insistent expression of someone used to getting her way.

"Nothing goes beyond this room?"

"Yes," I said. "Confidentiality is an ethical obligation."

She made a dismissive gesture with the back of her hand.

"I wasn't there, you understand, but I'll tell you what Nicky told me."

"Nicky?"

"Nicholas Grimes. His business partner."

"They owned the bank together?"

"Yes, they owned all of the stock."

"Was the ownership equal?"

"It was. It still is."

"They were the only ones on the boat?"

"Yes."

The questions had been simple, and the answers were crisp and without any tell-tale hesitation.

So far, so good.

"Alright."

I took out a pen and held it poised above a legal pad, waiting.

She resettled herself and restarted, like a person feeling for the truth, or some version of it, at least.

"Tarry and Nicky, Nick, were part of a social crowd going back to before they started the bank, a group of businessmen who keep power boats on the river. They take their boats up to Georgetown on Sunday afternoons all summer. They drop anchor and what they call, raft up."

"What do they do then?"

"Drink."

"What else?"

She shifted uncomfortably.

"They've been doing this since before Tarry and I got married. I don't ask too many questions. I don't really want to know, to tell the truth."

She knew alright, and I could imagine several possibilities. I'd noticed these power boats lashed together on summer afternoons, often a dozen or more together. On summer evenings, when I would sometimes hike the trails of Roosevelt Island looking for warblers, I could often hear the music and the raucous laughter.

"How come you don't go along to these parties?"

She made the gesture again with the back of her hand.

"It's a boys' thing. Besides, I don't like the water."

I believed her. She was too carefully made up and put together to risk her appearance to the wind a power boat can generate. I thought of Liz's observation that she'd be unlikely to ride to the hounds. Bobbitt was no sports-woman, but she was happy to reap the benefits of a country club marriage.

"Who owned the boat?"

"Nicky."

Nicky again.

"You're going to have to drop that Nicky stuff or people are going to begin asking questions."

"Nick. He keeps it down at the Pentagon Marina."

The Pentagon Marina was on the Virginia side of the river, just south of Memorial Bridge.

"What kind of boat is it?"

"I don't know, I just know it cost a lot of money."

I wondered how she knew that, but I didn't ask.

"Could your husband swim?"

"Of course. He's been around the water all of his life."

I waited and she resumed the story.

"Nick, some of the others, they miss it when the season's over. They're some hardy souls. For years now, they've marked each new year with a trip up to Georgetown for lunch at Bomba's Beach Shack. He gets Tarry to go because it's a good luck tradition. You know Bomba's?"

"Sure."

I had been there, but not on New Year's Day. It featured a Caribbean motif and live music and could be raucous even on a Tuesday afternoon.

"And they drink?"

She sighed dramatically.

"It's New Year's; they have a drink or two. If they didn't, they'd be the only ones."

I paused and decided to spare her a detailed recounting of what likely happened next. "And your husband wasn't on the boat when they got back to the marina?"

"Nick says he looked back when they passed under Memorial Bridge, and he was gone. That's all I know."

There were no tears from Bobbitt. If she was still affected nearly six months after her husband's disappearance, she didn't show it. Nor was there any display of unfelt sorrow.

Cool . . . or just plain cold?

"The obvious conclusion is that he drowned, but it's strange that no one found his body."

"There was a big storm that night," she said.

She moved a finger along her jaw and then between her teeth—the first emotion she had shown.

"So, if your husband's dead, Grimes gets the bank?"

"He'd have to buy his shares from me, but yes. I don't want them. The last thing I want is to be part owner of a bank. It's just a matter of settling on a price."

She seemed weary of the topic, but not troubled by it.

"The legal presumption is that Tarry's still alive. Was there a major change in your bank balances in, let's say the week after Christmas?"

"I have no idea. Tarry kept track of the finances and I didn't ask many questions."

"But that was six months ago."

"I've got a financial manager now."

"Where'd you find him?"

"Nick. He's a friend of Nicky's."

Alarm bells went off in my head.

"And you trust him?"

She shrugged.

"Nicky trusts him."

Something didn't smell right. She had a pat story, but the emotional angles didn't fit together.

"I'd like to put together some evidence."

Her brow furrowed.

"What kind of evidence?"

"I hate to put it this way, but evidence tending to show that your husband drowned."

She turned pensively toward the window.

"It's an unpleasant thought."

It wasn't the first painful image I'd floated, but only the second one that bothered her. "I'm sorry."

"But you think that would improve our chances to win?"

"Look at it this way. The statute speaks about the 'high seas.' The Potomac River is less than half a mile wide near Memorial Bridge, and it runs through one of the most heavily populated areas of the country. It would be hard to convince an Arlington County judge that the Potomac constitutes the high sea, but most judges are willing to stretch the law a little if they think justice is being served. Subconsciously, if the judge is convinced that your husband's dead, he or she will look for a way to arrive at a fair result, which would mean getting you out of this legal no man's land when everyone knows he's not coming back."

Bobbitt nodded, understanding the logic.

"I'd also like to get permission to look at your bank accounts."

She looked up sharply.

"I don't think that will be necessary. I came to you to have my husband declared dead, not to investigate my life."

"You're much more likely to get a positive ruling if the judge is convinced that we've looked at all the possibilities."

She took the message in stride, and I could see the wheels turning in her head.

"How much is that going to cost me?"

"I've got a guy who'll do the investigation for another $5,000."

"On top of what I pay you?"

"Yes."

"And how much is that?"

"Probably twenty, twenty-five thousand."

She screwed up her face into a look of extreme dismay.

"You know I don't have access to that kind of money. Not now. I will if we win."

I was sure Liz had quoted her a much higher figure. For a moment, I wondered if this was the real reason she had sent her to me.

"Can't you get a loan? You must know a good banker."

The comment didn't offend her.

"Nicky would help me if he could, but I'm not sure the rest of the bank board would back him up."

We went back and forth about the numbers before she agreed to a ten-thousand-dollar retainer and another five for the investigation.

That concluded, I escorted Bobbitt to the office door.

"One more thing. How much does your husband weigh?"

She looked me over.

"He's an average-sized man; tall and thin. Much smaller than you. A hundred and seventy or so. Why?"

I didn't answer. Instead, I again expressed my condolences. She nodded like I was commiserating over a dented fender.

Chapter Five

Qui Bono

I spent the next few minutes at my desk, running through the known facts and their likely implications. The first thing to consider was who benefited from the disappearance of Tarry Justice. That list might or might not include his wife, but it certainly included Nick Grimes, his business partner and the man who would soon become the sole owner of a prosperous bank. That's how the police and prosecutors would work it. That would have been their approach with Track, and I wondered, not for the first time, if they were still sifting through those possibilities. They must be considering who might benefit from Track's "disappearance."

It certainly isn't me.

***

Liz Hillman was a sharp lady, but I knew how to get her off her game. I picked up the phone and called her. I seemed to catch her between cigarettes.

"I met with your gal."

"How did that go?"

"I feel terrible for her. She seems quite distraught."

"Bobbitt? No, she's a tough bird."

"She certainly speaks highly of you."

"Does she? I haven't done anything for her."

"Except send her to me."

Liz laughed, as I intended.

"At least you convinced her that you have her best interests at heart. Have you been friends long?"

"Friends? I hardly know her."

"Oh? I got the impression that you were her divorce lawyer long before her husband fell off the boat."

"Oh, no. It doesn't sound like it was a particularly happy marriage, but they left each other alone, so she was content."

"Left each other alone? Were they living together?"

"Yes and no. They have a place in Arlington, but she spends most of her time at the Pelham. Not that it matters."

"Of course it matters. She came to you for a divorce."

"No, no. She came to me for closure. She didn't come in until last week."

"I see. When she learned about the lost-at-sea statute?"

"Something like that."

"I wonder who clued her into that?"

"Maybe Nick Grimes. I know he wants to get the bank ownership resolved."

Nick again. But that made sense. Without Justice around, they might not even have a quorum to do business.

"Any idea what she expects to do if she's declared a widow?"

"Probably take a deep breath and get on with her life. I don't think she's got any concrete plans, if that's what you mean."

I thanked her and hung up.

Liz was not by nature a curious person. She assembled evidence and put her cases together with the diligence of a beaver building a dam but gave little thought to what might lie hidden within the quirks and secret motivations of human nature.

But I knew somebody who did. I walked up the dimly lit wooden stairs to visit the lair of my longtime landlord.

DP Tran had owned the two-story, yellow brick office building on Wilson Boulevard since before I'd come to Arlington. He operated his various enterprises from a long, low, dingy room that occupied the entire upper floor of the building. While Twin Killings Investigations was dormant, Twin Killing Bail Bonds kept up a steady business.

His place was crowded with tools of his various trades: exercise equipment, a workbench featuring several disassembled locks, cameras and video equipment of all description.

It was a hot summer day, and I found him behind his desk, wearing a pale guayabera shirt, chin in hand and a distracted look on his round, often dour face. He had the stoic expression of a chronically underemployed man. Financially, he was scraping by like the rest of us, in his case, writing bail bonds for criminal defendants and tracing them when they skipped, collecting rent and earning fees for teaching t'ai chi to old ladies and kooks. He was making ends meet, but his mind was unengaged and that was both a waste and a tragedy.

"I think I've got some work for you."

DP looked at me like someone waiting for the punchline of a bad joke.

"What kind of work?"

"It's work that anyone can do legally, but it requires someone with your skill set to do it efficiently, delicately and right."

This was exactly what he wanted to hear—detective work by a different name. He tossed his head confidently.

"What do you want to know?"

That was his business: knowledge. More specifically, obtaining hard-to-find knowledge.

"If a guy named Tarry Justice is dead."

He tapped a finger on the side of his nose and repeated the name as if accessing his store of knowledge.

"What happened?"

"He fell off a boat into the Potomac River on New Year's Day and was never seen or heard from again."

He shut his eyes and repeated the name again.

"Tarry Justice. I remember hearing about that on the news. A couple of middle-aged men boating on New Year's Day. Freezing cold. The Commonwealth was suspicious."

"Heather's always suspicious when someone disappears."

I swallowed, remembering her reaction when Track Racker disappeared. But that had nothing to do with Justice, so I tugged at my ear and made myself focus.

"I don't know how much you remember," I said.

I assumed it was a lot because DP's mind was a depository of curious and unexplained facts.

"It was cold, and they'd been drinking and were probably in a hurry to get home."

He nodded as he pushed around the Asian-motif paper weights on his desk.

"Those little cruisers are noisy."

"Yeah, they are. If Grimes was focused on navigating the channel in the dark, he wouldn't necessarily have noticed if Justice lost his balance and fell overboard."

"Are you trying to prove that he's dead, or that he's *not* dead?"

"Dead," I said.

"You'll want to know the water temperature in the Potomac that evening. We need to know how long a person could survive in water that cold."

"He weighed a hundred and seventy pounds, if that'll help you."

"It does."

I briefly explained the facts as I understood them from Liz and Bobbitt. DP looked at a corner of the ceiling for a moment, seeming to gather his thoughts.

"How do you know Justice was ever on the boat?"

"Yeah, I had that reaction, too," I said. "The body didn't turn up and being married to Bobbitt doesn't seem like an attractive proposition, but divorce was an option for him, too, if he wanted one. And why would he walk away from a half interest in a thriving bank?"

"You're assuming the bank was making money."

"That's easy enough for you to check out."

He paused and the expression on his face tightened.

"There's another possibility," said DP. "A lot of un-secured debt. You know, the kind you don't wash off in bankruptcy."

I thought about Jimmie Flambeau, the man who had cornered the Arlington, Virginia market on off-the-books debt. There'd be a way to track that down, too, if it became important.

"No indication of that yet," I said. "So where do we start?"

He shook his head and looked at me with an expression of patience.

"Where we always do," said DP. "Who benefits?"

"Who benefits if he's dead?" I said.

It was the same question I'd asked myself.

DP shrugged.

"Bobbitt, of course," I said. "She wants closure."

"Virginia's a no-fault state," said DP. "She could have had a divorce if that's what she wanted. Was she seeking a divorce before her husband went missing?"

"No, Liz said she'd only come to her after learning of the lost-at-sea statute. She also implied that Grimes might have told her about it."

I waited, wanting to see if DP might have the same reaction I did.

"And he'll end up with the bank."

I nodded in agreement.

"That's a thought to tuck away." I said. "But for now, we just need to show he's dead."

DP was undeterred, DP was never deterred.

"The only reasons Liz Hillman would pass up a case is if there's no money in it or if it puts her at risk. Which is it?"

I thought about Liz's comment that Bobbitt would have money when the case was over.

"You'll get paid. You don't need to worry about that. I was hired to prove that my client's husband was lost at sea. Let's leave it at that."

"Okay."

He asked a few follow-up questions and listened carefully to my answers. DP never wrote anything down, but he absorbed facts like a sponge. This was one of the reasons I liked working with him: there was never any record of what was said between us.

"I'll snoop around," he said.

"She's not paying you to snoop around. She just wants to win the case."

A grin lit up his pie-shaped face. DP was just like me and that's why we got along. He couldn't let a loose thread go.

"When do you need this?"

"Tomorrow afternoon? Is that too soon?"

"Not a problem."

I went back to my office. A few minutes later, I heard the front door open and close. I pulled back the blind and peered out the window on an afternoon bright with early summer sun. There was DP, hands plunged into the pockets of his cargo pants and head down, striding down Wilson Boulevard to access whatever sources he could use to find the answers to my questions.

DP Tran was a curious man who was always fitting pieces together. I wondered if Terry Justice's apparent drowning has turned his thoughts to the unexplained disappearance of Track Racker.

Chapter Six

DP Delivers

When DP stepped into my office the next morning, he looked grim. He sat down and struck a thoughtful pose.

"What did you find out?"

"Some things to chew over. What you might not understand about Bobbitt and Tarry is that they didn't much like each other, but they had a solid marriage for a number of years."

"You're right. I didn't understand that. And I don't understand what you're talking about."

He crossed one leg over the opposite knee and put a finger to the tip of his nose.

"Not everyone wants peace and harmony in a marriage. Some people thrive on the daily battle of wills: love as a zero-sum game. Some of those people are able to maintain that tension for years, even for decades of living together."

I had never been married and I practiced law alone, but I was familiar with the challenges inherent in human co-existence. After all, I was a trial lawyer.

"The problem with that is, over time, someone usually wins, and someone loses."

"Sooner or later, sure. And when that happens, the loser gets fed up and the winner gets bored. But that can take years of misery to play out."

I thought of Liz Hillman's first law partner, a charming but insecure personal lawyer who had been married and divorced four times and who had a chronic inability to ignore perceived slights. Placid waters made him suspicious and uneasy, so he looked for excuses to stir the pot. This trait made him a fine lawyer, but marriage and partnership had proved impossible for him.

"And the Justices were one of those couples?"

"Yeah. Now, I don't know how far they had gotten on the continuum, but maybe that marriage had run its course."

"Does it matter?"

"No, because Justice was on the boat. And he drowned. At least everyone I've talked to is convinced of it."

"What about you?"

He shrugged.

"It's hard to see any other explanation that fits the facts."

"How can you be so sure?"

"This winter power boat group, there were about a dozen of them, and they called themselves the Snowmen. They had lunch every year on New Year's Day at Bomba's. The tradition goes back seven or eight years. Justice was there last January, and he was drunk. You don't get drunk before pulling off a disappearing act."

"How do you know he was drunk?"

He ignored the question.

"Not only that; he had a half-dozen lines of cocaine in him."

"Cocaine? That surprises me."

"They didn't call themselves the Snowmen because they got together on New Year's Day each year."

"Really? Now, that changes things a bit, doesn't it?"

"Does it? He's still dead."

"True."

I refocused, but I couldn't shake this new development.

"Did Justice have a cocaine problem?"

"Define a 'cocaine problem.' I know Grimes used it regularly. I assume they both did."

"So, he was drunk and high . . . enough to fall off a fast-moving boat in the dark?"

"You're the one who knows about boats."

I did, and I knew it was easy enough for a drunk to fall off a fast-moving boat in broad daylight.

"What kind of boat was it?"

"Twenty-two-foot Denali Pursuit."

I whistled.

"The one with the three hundred horse-power engine?"

"You know your boats."

"I know that one."

"I got a look at it at the marina today."

DP called up a photo on his phone and showed it to me.

"Yeah, that's it."

I knew the boat because a friend of mine in Boston had one: streamlined, fast and maneuverable . . . and expensive.

"Beautiful boat."

He cocked his head to study the photo.

"The cockpit's pretty deep and roomy. Looks like it would be hard to fall out of it."

"Ten to one when they find the body, they find him with his fly open."

"Huh?"

"He climbed up on the transom to take a leak and lost his balance. That's how it figures. You'd be surprised how often male bodies floating face down are recovered with their fly open. Okay, what else you got?"

He shuffled through the papers in his lap and handed me a dated table of water temperatures for the Potomac River, certified by an official of the National Oceanic and Atmospheric Administration. The temperature of the Potomac on the evening of New Year's Day was between 35 and 40 degrees Fahrenheit.

"Now we just have to figure out how long a drunk, 170-pound man can survive in water that cold," I said.

"Not more than an hour and a half without a life jacket."

"How do you know that?"

DP pulled out another sheet of paper and pushed it toward me. It was the *curriculum vitae* of a professor of medicine at George Washington University.

"Who's this guy?"

I glanced through some impressive credentials: Johns Hopkins and John Hopkins Med school. Internship at Brigham and Women's in Boston and a residency at Mass General.

"He's the guy who's prepared to testify to what I just said. If the money's is right."

"You did a lot in twenty-four hours."

He grinned. Like anyone else, DP enjoyed it when good work was acknowledged.

"I'm not done yet. Grimes has his own issues. And a girlfriend named Bonnie Blank. What a name, huh? He lets her live on less than market rent in a place he owns up in Lewes, Delaware. That can't be cheap."

"He's married, isn't he?"

"Sure is, although I don't know how long that'll last if this blows up."

"A girl friend in Delaware kind of undercuts the idea that he's involved with Bobbitt."

"I'm not sure about that. He sounds like an opportunist and Bobbitt sounds like an opportunity."

"Or maybe she saw Grimes as an opportunity to take a swipe at her husband. Either way, this is getting more expensive all the time. It means Grimes is going to want his partner's bank stock."

"Yeah. Early indications are that the bank makes money. They aren't killing it, but it isn't something a sane man would walk away from. Unless . . ."

"What?"

"Cocaine users have a way of running up debt."

"Any evidence that Justice was carrying off the books debt?"

"That's not the kind of thing that's easy to know."

"You think Jimmie Flambeau might know something about that?"

"I wouldn't bet against it. Especially because Flambeau and Nick Grimes have something in common."

"What's that?"

"They go to the same church."

I knew where Flambeau went to church, or at least claimed to.

"St. Carolyn's?"

He nodded.

"Don't you know someone over there?"

Chapter Seven

Mea Culpas

I knew several parishioners at St. Carolyn's Roman Catholic Church in Arlington, but the only one I was interested in seeing was Melanie Freeman.

Melanie had made it through forty years of life by taking full advantage of the extraordinary good looks God had given her. Now, with her beauty fading, she'd found a friend in Jesus. That was okay with me, and I wasn't above working a social relationship to help uncover the facts of a case. My three-day probationary period without a drink had passed, so I called her. She didn't seem surprised to hear my voice. She tended to believe that lost sheep return to the fold.

"I want to apologize for the other day," I said.

"You had been drinking?"

She'd have probably taken either answer, but I decided to give her the truth.

"It hasn't been a habit and I don't want to make it one."

"What happened?"

"You have a similar problem . . ."

"*Had.* I beat it every day."

"Yeah, well, I don't want it to get to that level with me. I know the first thing I'm supposed to do is to apologize to anyone I've hurt."

I heard her swallow.

"I appreciate it, Joth. It's not necessary."

I felt my way toward the appropriate tone.

"We've drifted apart, Melanie. Maybe that's the way it was going to be, I don't know. And I'm not interested in returning to the church, but we should stay friends."

"I think we *are* friends."

"Are you working tomorrow?"

She paused, this time to consider the implications of her answer.

"Yes. I've got the late shift. Three to ten."

That was perfect. Lunch would work a lot better than dinner for what I had in mind.

"Are you available for lunch?"

"I think I can do that."

"There's a new Vietnamese place in Ballston I've been meaning to try. Pick you up around noon?"

She agreed. I'd lied a little about wanting to try a new restaurant. I'd been to Saigon Breeze several times. DP's uncle owned it.

I spent the next day with an empty calendar, thinking through Bobbitt's problem and the diverse paths that could lead me to the truth. The office phone outside rang and rang. I was about to give Marie a piece of my mind when I realized it was her day off. I answered it, slightly annoyed at myself.

"Hi."

I was glad to hear Melanie's cheerful voice.

"I'm a little behind. I wonder of you'd pick me up over here?"

"Where's over here?"

I assumed it was the Del Ray assisted living facility home where she worked.

"I'm at the church. Just finishing up some volunteer work."

"You're at St. Carolyn's?"

"Yes. So, if it's not out of your way . . ."

Melanie's soul-saving motives were never far from the surface, so her being at the church seemed to be more than a coincidence. But St. Carolyn's was less out of my way than her apartment or Del Ray, so what the hell . . .

"Reserved for Father John."

I parked in his spot. As I pushed through the glass doors of the church offices, I found the reception area empty and made my way down the hall, where Melanie was laboring behind a computer station in a small, windowless office, inputting data. On the other side of the desk sat Father John Tedesco. The last time I'd seen him, I'd dropped him with one punch at the foot of a statute of St. Francis of Assisi.

Unlike the nave, a church office is not designed to over-awe the sinner or inspire the saint. Being in Father John's presence did not make me feel the intimidating presence of the Lord. It was a spare room, heavy on iconography of a modernistic bent: a stylized Pieta and op art renderings of familiar New Testament scenes. Green plants and bouquets of summer flowers set a sedate tone.

John, wearing a back, short sleeved shirt with a Roman collar, stood respectfully when I walked in. He nodded formally with his hands folded behind his back, awaiting my reaction like a biblical martyr awaiting the emperor's sentence. I stepped forward and extended my hand and as he took it, he smiled.

"It's been a while," he said.

Father John was undistinguished looking: medium height, unthreatening, and clean shaven, with dark hair and a habitually benign expression. His appearance was easy to forget, but also easy to trust.

He and I had our differences, but he was Jenny Tedesco's brother, and I knew that his sister's death could provide the impetus for a healing process between us. I had lashed out at him during my phone call with Melanie. I wasn't ready to trust him because my instincts told me not to, but the virtue of forgiveness was deeply engrained in me. It had been less than two months since I caught him embezzling from the woman who was now inputting data into the church computer across from him. It felt like two lifetimes ago.

"I owe you an apology," John said.

He was making an admirable display of Christian humility, but Melanie was the one he owed an apology! That said, I was exhausted and wanted to put all of that behind me. I was also conscious of a spiritual need, which Father John might have been able to fill. I was a man whose actions demanded atonement and redemption.

"Water under the bridge," I said.

I was ready to move on and if he was willing to put it all in the rearview mirror, that was okay with me.

"I'm not asking you for forgiveness. No doubt I'm in need of it, but that comes from a higher authority."

He pointed toward the ceiling and briefly raised his eyes in a practiced gesture of piety. In fact, I heard in his words a sincerity that his gesture toward the heavens only undercut.

"I did something stupid. Something selfish and I regret it. I'm glad you stopped me when you did."

He glanced at Melanie to make sure she had heard his bid for redemption.

Priests lived to set themselves up as the example of the lesson; it appealed to the martyr in them. While I couldn't shake a lingering distrust, he was presenting himself as the model of a man facing up to and atoning for his mistakes.

Having seen countless defendants mouth well-rehearsed platitudes to sentencing judges, I appreciated the simplicity of his statement. It was only by his example that I found it in myself to do the same thing.

"I made mistakes, too. Mistakes a lot worse than yours."

Father John also knew when to let it go. He glanced again at Melanie.

"The two of you have plans. I don't want to hold you up."

We shook hands again, needlessly, but with an exchange of personal regard that had been absent from the first effort.

"Stop by if you're in the area" he said. "I have a feeling we'll find a lot of talk about."

It was true. Although I had deep Puritan roots, I had been raised Catholic. Long ago lapsed, I intended to remain that way, but I'd been in love with his sister. There was room for us to bond over that connection.

Melanie had worked ceaselessly through this exchange, and I took the seat John had occupied to allow her to reach a stopping point. I assumed she had used our date as a pretense to get me into Father John's presence and I felt a small tinge of resentment. Neither my soul nor my relationship with her priest was her business, but I also knew she'd stay on it with the resolve of a mother of a reluctant altar boy.

And I knew she'd stick with me for the same reason—because she saw me as a project, someone to be redeemed. This was also the reason we had no future.

"He's not a bad sort," she said.

Her face puckered as she squinted at the computer screen.

"No, he's not."

"He's got a big and difficult job."

"I'm well aware of that. He's not only a shepherd to his flock; he's a politician."

Melanie looked up from the computer, confused.

"Family. He calls it his family. And I wouldn't say he's a politician."

She had come to understand that she was susceptible to the influence of strong men. I'd taught her that. As a result, she was becoming a careful, prudent woman.

"Don't kid yourself. Look at the different sorts of people he deals with to hold a community together. That's what good politicians do."

She wiggled uncomfortably in her chair. She had a nice way of wiggling. Although she had never told me directly, I had picked up clues as to why a woman as physically attractive as Melanie could remain unmarried into her forties. It wasn't the drinking, although that couldn't have helped, or the devotion to Catholic rituals, which was likely the effect, not the cause of her continued unmarried status. It was because she had been hard on men. I knew the type. She had to be that way as a mechanism to rebuff the consistent and unwelcome attentions that a woman as pretty as Melanie must have had to fend off on a daily basis throughout her younger years. Otherwise, she'd have had no peace because beautiful women never do.

That was the one positive I saw from her commitment to the church: the humility and the abandonment of her physical self-absorption had paradoxically made her more attractive. But the convert's zeal was a little hard for me to swallow.

Melanie had the administrative skills that any parish would want in a volunteer and Father John was a man with a sharp eye for benevolent talent.

"What's John got you doing back here? Data input?"

She took this as an innocent question, a digression from the potentially troubling discussion of John, his methods, and his motives.

"It's more than that. He has me organizing the parish into various subgroups."

"Based on what?"

"You know, people with a flair for drama tend toward the Christmas and Easter stuff, so we get them involved in the pageants. Those with taste are obvious recruits for the altar guild."

This observation gave me an idea.

"People with big money might be big donors?"

She huffed at the insinuation of a mercenary motive.

"It's alright," I said. "My mother did the same job when I was growing up. Our church was looking for the same things you are."

She looked up and smiled.

"I wonder where she pegged you?"

"The wrong place," I said. "But this helps you get to know the parish and the people in it, right?"

"Yes. It's really become my community. Father John thinks of it as his family. I hope I get to that point, too."

The lightbulb in my head glowed.

"I wonder if you know my old buddy, Nick Grimes?"

"Nick Grimes," she said, pursing her lips to recall. "Not really. I know who he is."

"He and I go way back. We used to play poker together every Saturday night before he made it big. He
owns a bank now and he's making a fortune. I'll bet
you've got him on the high donor list."

"I wouldn't know," she said.

She sounded wary, but I watched her scrolling
through the screen for a moment until her eyes blinked in
surprise.

"I'm sorry. I'm both nosy and impertinent sometimes. It's just that I heard that they run the bank board
on Coca-Cola and cocaine."

"Who told you that, Joth?"

"I wouldn't say it's common knowledge, but it's out
there."

"Well, I don't believe it."

She hadn't moved off the information she'd found.
She looked troubled and her brow furrowed again.

"Joth, are you okay?"

"I don't know."

I slumped in the chair.

"Just a momentary thing, I'm sure."

I groaned and placed my hand on my chest. Melanie
got up and came around the desk, but I held up my other
hand to keep her away.

"I'm alright. Do you think you could get me a glass
of water?"

"Of course."

She turned and hurried for the door.

"And maybe a damp cloth and some aspirin?"

"Of course. I'll be right back."

As soon as she was gone, I slid around the desk to view the computer. My hunch was right. Her curiosity had gotten the better of her and she'd brought Nick Grimes's information up. He had a history as a big donor alright, but in recent years he'd met his pledges only sporadically, with nothing at all in the past twelve months. I was back in my chair, feigning illness again, when Melanie returned with a paper cup, a wet washcloth, and two aspirin.

She put the cloth on my forehead.

"You feel alright," she said.

I took the aspirin and swallowed them with the water.

"Yeah, whatever it was seems to have passed. I haven't eaten and I'm probably just a little faint."

She looked at her watch.

"Oh dear, I forgot about lunch. We can go. I can finish this later."

Following her to the door, I slowed enough to swing around for one more peek at the computer screen, but she turned and caught me and slapped my hand as if I were a naughty child. "I like to check up on my friends," I said.

She snapped off the monitor.

"Well, you're nosy."

"Everybody says that. Yes, I suppose I am."

***

Saigon Breeze was in a strip mall in Ballston, one of Arlington's emerging business hubs. Melanie, being ever trustful, was prone to accept facts that tracked her predisposition, so on the drive over I convinced her that my recovery had been as complete as it was swift, and she became both talkative and attentive. I felt a little more than a twinge of guilt for duping her as I had and resolved to make it up to her with an enjoyable lunch and maybe something else afterward.

The hostess found us a quiet table amid a light crowd composed mostly of businesspeople. I guided the conversation from innocent starter topics to what I hoped were suggestive inquiries to see if she'd bite. She missed the subtext, or at least acted like she did, and studied the menu with a perplexed frown.

"Try the ginger chicken, Melanie."

She closed the menu. She was a woman who liked men to make decisions for her and for that reason I worried about her and Father John—not because I saw him as a sexual predator, but as something worse, a ghoul who was after her soul.

I threw out another fishing line.

"I was glad Father John left us alone. He must trust my intentions."

She looked up inquisitively and smiled, with no idea what I was hinting at.

"He's not a bad sort. He's a man who has faced up to his shortcomings. I admire that. But he has demons like everyone else."

She had turned the conversation to a difficult subject. I knew that any relationship that included or touched on Father John would necessarily be fraught. My older brother Edward had been an altar boy and he'd been abused by a Catholic priest. Ned took his own life on his twentieth birthday. I had difficulty feeling sympathy for Father John's challenges, but I persisted.

"What kind of demons?"

"For one thing, he wants to know what happened to his sister."

The point made me uncomfortable, which she noticed.

"I can understand that."

"He thinks you're holding back to punish him. He'd appreciate it if you'd open up a little about it."

"What makes him think I know anything about what happened to his sister?"

"You were dating her."

"We broke up."

"But not long before. And now, you won't talk about it? He's not the only person wondering."

"Does that mean you?"

"He thinks you know what happened. I think you do, too, but it doesn't really matter to me. To him, it's different."

"He knows what happened to Jenny. She died."

"You didn't even show up for the funeral."

"That's true. I should have. I was too angry."

"You seem to get angry a lot."

"I try not to."

I wondered how I'd gone from come-on lines to confessing to the failure of good intentions.

"How did she die?"

"I don't know."

"Frank Racker was your client. Some people think he knows."

"He might."

"Then, why aren't your helping the police find him?"

I stared at her for a long moment. I had never thought of it that way before. Perhaps the reason the police were so focused on me was because they thought I was hiding a guilty client.

"Maybe you two aren't so different after all, you and Father John. Just two lonely guys trying to find meaning in life. I don't think you'll find the same answer. And that's all right. But I think each of you might help the other find his own answer."

The food came and Melanie ate in the comfortable silence of one used to eating alone. Or perhaps she intended to let the ideas she had seeded germinate in me. She was a more complex woman than she appeared, or perhaps it was just that I had once again underestimated the qualities often hidden within a pretty woman.

Through the rest of the meal, our conversation veered toward the sort of banal and harmless topics she seemed to prefer: the latest sitcom, new self-help books and rom-com movies she'd like to see.

After lunch, I dropped her off at her apartment. I thanked her and didn't ask to come in. It just didn't seem like the right time for dessert.

Chapter Eight

Playing Detective

The information disclosed by Melanie, along with what I gleaned from the church computer data, sat heavily with me. Something about what I'd learned kept me from dropping it, or at least leaving it buried on a mental shelf somewhere—a sure sign that I sensed more than I understood. Late in the day, I took my hunch up to DP's office. He was behind his desk, engrossed in paperwork and I took the chair across from him and waited for him to look up.

"Did you find out anything about the cocaine Tarry Justice got into on New Year's Day?"

"A little bit," he said. "It was passed around pretty freely that day at Bomba's."

"How do you know?"

"Because somebody called the police. They showed up and busted a guy named Lincoln Charlestraton."

"Lincoln Charlestraton?"

"Yeah, pretty common name."

He looked at me wryly.

"No, I've heard that name before."

I searched my memory bank but came up empty.

"What's he look like?"

"I didn't see him, but I put the same question to Bomba."

DP took a request for a description like a spot check of his professional diligence. He pursed his lips and called up the information from his memory.

"Black guy, younger than us, has a beard. Slim and athletic."

"But you didn't talk to him?"

"Didn't have to."

He swiveled to a filing cabinet, pulled open the top drawer and removed a manilla folder, flipped through it, and took out a thin sheaf of documents, which he pushed across the desk.

"What's this?"

"A copy of the notes of the investigating officer at Charlestraton's arrest."

"How did you get these?"

"You don't want to know."

He gave me several pages of typewritten notes that looked like they had been hurriedly photographed through a cell phone. Each shot was a poorly centered section of a partial page. I stopped on one with Charlestraton's name at the top and scanned through.

"Possession with intent to distribute and distribution of a controlled substance."

I looked up at DP.

"Yeah, they caught him with a couple of gram vials in the glove box of his car. The indication is that he'd already sold one to Justice."

"Where did that information come from?"

He leaned forward and moved the pages about like pieces of a jigsaw puzzle and tapped a line with his index finger.

"That he sold one to Justice? The sentence is broken between two screen shots, but that's what Grimes said."

I looked where he was reading.

"Grimes's statement is dated January 3. That was two days after the arrest. Justice had already disappeared."

"Yeah, nothing like throwing your partner under the bus when the cops come around asking hard questions."

"Or when your partner's not around to contest the facts."

DP stroked his chin.

"That tells us one thing. Grimes must have believed Justice was dead."

"Not much doubt about that. I wonder what else he believed?"

"I'll tell you what I believe," DP said. "Grimes was having money problems and so was the bank."

"How do you know that?"

"I confirmed the girlfriend in Lewes, and a young, sweet thing she is. They don't come cheap."

"How 'bout the bank?"

He hunched his narrow shoulders.

"From what I could find, they started out fine. Both Justice and Grimes had built solid reputations in the banking community for their hard work and smarts, and they really milked that William and Mary network. They were in the black by the second year, but then they got greedy. They started making high interest loans on risky real estate deals. Some of those deals went south and other investors started to get nervous. You know how that goes once it gets started."

I did. Business shortfalls can be like gambling debts, pushing the debtor to double down to get out of the hole, with each new bet dicier than the one before it.

"The bank's failing?"

"No, far from it. But they were going to have to make some hard decisions even before Justice went missing."

"Hard decisions can be tough to make when they require two people to agree."

"Yup. That may explain some things. Or it might not."

I told him what I'd found out about Grimes.

"You think Justice was also having money problems?" he said.

"I don't know. But I know how to find out."

***

I knew someone else who attended St. Carolyn's, or had once claimed to. If there was one person in Arlington who had his hand on the pulse of the social vices that preyed on the county's high rollers, it was Jimmie Flambeau—gambler, bookie and lender of last resort.

Only a handful of people knew where Jimmie lived or worked and one of them was Irish Dan Crowley, the proprietor of a Crystal City gentlemen's club, called Riding Time.

Dan was a long-standing referral source and sometime client. Jenny Tedesco, Father John's sister, had worked for Irish Dan as a dancer, using the working name, Jade. She had made plans to get out of that scene and when those plans came to fruition, she became Jenny again. She'd been admitted to nursing school at my *alma mater* and was on her way to a new life when she died, or should I say, was killed. Since then, I hadn't been inside the club.

The throbbing backbeat of bass-heavy music was audible from the sidewalk. Inside, the smell of sweat and stale beer, along with the claustrophobic heat, revived unwelcome memories. A blonde woman I didn't recognize was working the main pole and another newbie was in the cage on the small stage in back.

I found a stool at the bar and ordered a draft from a heavy-set female bartender with purple hair and a sleeve of tattoos up both arms. Before she could draw my beer, Irish Dan, always attentive to the moods and needs of his clientele, appeared across from me, his big, ruddy face alive with good cheer. He shook my hand with characteristic warmth.

Dan was an old friend and a good one. By staying away from him, I had only been punishing myself. He took the draft from the bartender, poured it down the sink, and drew a new one from a different tap. He slid it across the wooden bar.

"This is a pilsner from a new brewery in Baltimore. It's the best we serve," he said, with a wink. "How are you. Counselor?"

I lifted the glass in salute and put it back down without tasting it.

"I've been better."

"I was sorry about Jade," he said, still using Jenny's working name.

Dan was measuring my reaction carefully. I barely nodded.

"I was surprised I didn't see you at the funeral."

DP was one of the few people I could open up to. Dan was another.

"I should have been there, Dan. It was just too much."

"Her brother was there. Maybe you should talk to him."

"Father John? I thought you didn't trust him?"

He shrugged in his good-natured way.

"People change."

"Don't tell me he's become a patron of this place?"

Dan stuck up for the underdog with the instincts of a public defender. He turned his beefy palms upward.

"He's a complicated guy."

"The priesthood doesn't have room for complicated guys."

He fastened his big blue eyes on me, then reached for my mug and took a sip. He looked at me steadily.

"Don't underestimate him, Joth. He's a different kind of priest. He was one of those guys who joined not to save souls but to change the world."

He read my expression.

"Yeah, he wanted to protest against the war, fight against poverty, and organize sit-ins for racial justice. All that sort of stuff."

I was dubious.

"How do you know that?"

"His sister told me."

I pulled the beer back and took a long drink.

"What happened?"

"I don't know. Jade knew, but she wouldn't say."

"You been talking to him?"

He shrugged.

"He was in here trying to find out what happened to his sister."

"He should let it go."

"You've been trying to do the same thing, haven't you?"

"A little. The police haven't really focused on it like they should and that bothers me."

"It bothers John, too. He wonders why."

I sighed.

"They'll get involved just enough to muddy up the trail."

"That's usually what happens," he said.

Dan used a cloth to mop the bar as he gathered his thoughts. He knew I wasn't there for the entertainment.

"What can I do for you today?"

"I'm looking for Jimmie Flambeau. I thought you might know where I could find him."

Dan smiled as if we were sharing an inside joke. Jimmie Flambeau didn't turn out for just anyone. Those he made book for usually dealt with his minions. And those who owed him money *always* dealt with his minions.

He looked at me sympathetically.

"Trying to get a bet down?

"I need some information."

"You usually come to me for that."

"Not for this."

He looked rueful.

"I can tell him you're looking for him. Anything specific?"

"Yeah, about six months ago, a guy named Tarry Justice fell off a boat in the Potomac and disappeared. I want to know if he owed anybody money."

"Anybody meaning Jimmie."

"That's right."

Dan put his fingertips to his lips.

"You don't mind taking chances, do you?"

"It's an innocent question."

"I'm not sure Jimmie's going to agree."

I pulled a business card out of my jacket pocket and slid it onto the bar. Dan pushed it back at me.

"Jimmie knows where to find you. If he wants to."

I got up to go.

"And Joth, one more thing. There was a bull in here yesterday, asking questions."

"This is a busy place, isn't it?"

"Sometimes."

"Questions about what?"

"About Frank Racker."

I nodded.

"Heavy set guy with a flat top?

"That's him."

"Name of Anderson?"

He pulled a business card from his shirt pocket to check the name.

"That's the guy."

He offered me the card, but I waved it away.

"Who did he talk to?"

He shrugged.

"People around here tend to clam up when a cop walks in. But somebody gave him Gala's name."

Gala Thompson had been Jenny's roommate. Track Racker owed Gala money from an insurance payout and the arsenic that had killed Jenny had been intended for her, although the police never tied it to her. I knew that she tended bar at Dan's sports pub just up the street.

"What time does she come on?"

"I wouldn't worry about her. She wouldn't be a reliable witness against anybody."

I knew what he meant. What I didn't understand is how Dan could continue to employ someone with such an obvious substance abuse problem. But the answer came to me almost as quickly as the question. Dan was a soft touch, and he was afraid of what might happen to Gala if he cut her loose.

"She live in the same place?"

"Yup. I haven't found her a new roommate yet."

"What time does she start her shift at the pub?"

He looked at his watch.

"She's working right now."

***

Gala Thompson and Jenny had shared a tidy, two-bedroom duplex in Del Ray. They weren't friends, but they were making their way through life on parallel tracks. Dan liked to keep his girls together and liked it even better when they paid him rent.

The Washington Sports Pub occupied the first floor of a former warehouse space, just up the street from Riding Time. On a hot afternoon in early summer, it was sparsely filled with a lot of the same crew who'd move on to Dan's other place after they'd knocked back enough beers or watched enough baseball. The five big screen TVs were all showing a Cubs home game. Three of the five pool tables were busy, and a teenager was pumping quarters into a video machine in a corner by the restroom.

In the back, under a bank of track lights, Gala stood behind the copper-topped bar, messaging on her cell phone. I pulled up a stool and waited for her to notice me. When she looked up, I asked for a draft. She nodded and turned to draw it. I'd met her a handful of times including once when I'd used a lost gloves ruse to squeeze some information from her about Track Racker, but she didn't seem to know me from the Prince of Wales. I guessed that she didn't remember a lot of things. That would make it easy, or so I thought.

Gala had a pretty face but was pale, overly made up, and had the drooping eyes of someone not fully engaged. She showed an armful of tattoos as she slid me the beer.

"A little slow today."

"A little slow," she said.

It sounded as if a rote reply was all she could muster. She turned away without making eye contact and returned to her phone. I was considering my approach when someone slid onto the stool next to me.

"Are you buying, Counselor?"

Detective Anderson was wearing the same cheap blue blazer he had on during his visit to my office.

"Maybe you ought to be buying, Detective. You can expense it. I can't."

"Oh, I'm sure you can find some way to bill this to an unsuspecting client. If you have any clients."

I turned back to my beer and the Cubs game. I had an advantage over Anderson because I knew what he was doing there, but he was free to do what cops do best: assume whatever fit best with his preconceived notions.

He nodded at Gala, and she brought him a beer.

"You know this lady?"

Gala looked at me without a hint of recognition.

"Ask her if she knows me," I said.

She turned away as if she hadn't heard a word and I was grateful for small blessings. He seemed surprised.

"So, what are you doing here?'

"I could ask you the same thing, Detective. At least I'm not drinking on the public dime."

Anderson smiled and I could see in his eyes that he liked my answer. Most people who crack wise to a cop can expect to get hit sooner or later and I was pushing my luck.

He looked again at Gala. If I was here conspiring with her on a cover story, it would fit neatly with his developing theory about Track Racker's disappearance, but Gala's inability to recognize me put a chill on his expectations. I also saw that I'd already gotten what I'd come here to find out. Gala wasn't going to sell me out.

She didn't even remember who I was. That was the way she lived, and I suppose she had to.

I pushed my beer away.

"It smells like a rat died under the bar. Tell the waitress to fumigate this place, will you?"

I got up off my stool and nodded toward my unfinished beer.

"You can pick this up, Anderson. Put it on your expense account."

***

Two afternoons later, late in the day, I looked up as an extremely large human blocked the light in the doorway to my office. We'd met before. It was Felipe Pasquale, Jimmie Flambeau's principal goon.

"I understand you want to see Mr. Flambeau."

He spoke slowly, with a grave rumble in his voice. I wasn't sure if this was an affectation of toughness or if he was really the moron he seemed to be.

"Word gets around."

"Let's go. You're driving."

Felipe was black haired, swarthy and heavy through the jaw and jowls. He wore the thug persona like a Halloween costume: a cheaply tailored green blazer, silk pants and a pair of handstitched loafers that probably cost as much as the rest of his outfit.

As I drove, he watched me with hooded eyes, as if measuring me for the fight that we both assumed was sure to come. I didn't relish it, but it didn't scare me either. I took a long look at his jacket.

"I didn't know you'd won the Masters."

His eyes shifted to the windshield.

"Just drive," he said.

The trip was short, and I was grateful. Felipe was a looming and oppressive presence with body odor that could kill a rodent, and he didn't say another word beyond a series of terse and monosyllabic directions. We pulled up at Fort C. S. Smith, a county green space that was once a part of a series of Civil War-era installations, known as the Arlington Line. Other than a few cannons, some eroded trenches and an historic house, there were few reminders of the old fort or the war. These days, it was frequented mostly by birdwatchers, dog walkers, and joggers. I stepped out of the car into a humid, windless summer afternoon, which limited visitors to a handful.

Felipe directed me through a gap in the rail fence. At the top of the rise was a gazebo-like structure built around an old stone well. Behind it were a pair of wooden benches. Jimmie Flambeau sat on one of them.

Flambeau reminded me of a goalie who had bedeviled me in high school and then again in college for four straight years. Blaine Cox was compact, loose-jointed, and quick as a flash. In the off season, I'd see him periodically and he always appeared relaxed and at ease, except for a steely intensity that never left his blue eyes and that betrayed his easy-going personal style. In truth, Blaine Cox was an assassin who could lull you to sleep before plunging the knife.

Flambeau had the same hypnotic eyes. He dressed like Cox did away from the field: white tennis shorts and a purple Banlon shirt, open at the neck one button more than it should be. On the little finger of his right hand, he wore a yellow diamond in a platinum setting. He didn't have the type of hands you'd want to call attention to: small, with crooked fingers, which suggested a life of broken bones.

Jimmie's face had seen some ragged miles, too, but he still maintained some vestiges of youth. He wasn't the sort of person to acknowledge the fraying of the aging process. I wondered what sports he had played. He looked like he had been a formidable competitor in his day.

Felipe led me to him like he was leading a captured Confederate courier to the officer of the day. Flambeau looked me over through his blue tinted sunglasses. The word on Jimmie was that he never smiled. He was smiling now and that made me nervous.

"Hey, you've lost weight since the last time I saw you. Working out?"

The last time I'd seen him, Felipe and another Flambeau thug tried to brace me in a hotel room at Jimmie's direction. They didn't get what they were looking for, but I did.

"Cutting out the gluten."

"I hear that's good for you. I also hear you want some information."

A pair of cardinals in a Japanese maple tree were cheeping. Otherwise, the park was as quiet as death.

"I figured it can't hurt to ask."

"Oh, it can hurt, Counselor. You ought to know that."

"I'm a slow learner."

"Yeah. I hear you're still kind of sweet on that cute prosecutor."

"We're friends."

"The kind of friend where she might ask you to do her a favor?"

"She might. But I'm not stupid enough to wear a wire."

He gestured to his minion.

"Feel him up, Felipe."

Felipe had a pair of hands like a blacksmith, and he frisked me quickly, efficiently and with no pretense of delicacy.

"Nothin'."

I tucked the tail of my shirt back into my pants and Flambeau motioned toward an adjacent bench. I ignored the invitation and remained standing.

"Okay, what do you need?"

He asked, as if the Kabuki dance with Felipe had not taken place and meeting him here was just a coincidence.

"I want to know if a banker named Tarry Justice owes you any money."

"Tarry Justice? He's dead, isn't he?"

"I don't know. Some people think he is."

"Why do you think he might owe me money?"

"Because he dropped a lot of money on cocaine."

Flambeau lifted his sunglasses to take a probing look at me.

"You take a big swing. I like that."

"A lot of people don't. Look Jimmie, I know drugs isn't your thing, but people who get behind sometimes come to you for a little short-term financial assistance."

He studied me for a long moment, then nodded his head.

"Tarry Justice," he said.

He settled back into the bench as a lawn mower started up at the south end of the park. The noise startled him, and he looked up. In that moment, I understood that it was tough to be Jimmie Flambeau. Recognizing the sound, he recaptured his casual persona.

"The cocaine thing surprises me. Kind of a Boy Scout from what I know."

"The DC police have a guy under arrest for selling him a vial of cocaine."

He shook his head judiciously.

"I don't think so. Like I told you, he's a Boy Scout. Or was."

"Doesn't gamble?"

"Not with me. Now his partner . . ."

"Nick Grimes."

He looked up at me with a convivial smile.

"You know anything about Nick Grimes?"

"I know he goes to your church."

"Yeah, I heard you had problems over there, Counselor."

"I don't get along with the priest."

He laughed.

"Me neither."

"Then how come you go?"

Flambeau clicked his tongue.

"The real question is, how come you *don't* go? It's wise to keep your fire insurance paid up."

"You think that's gonna work?"

"I'm just a careful guy."

He sat back on the bench, took his glasses off and let the sun warm his face.

"Now, let me see if I've got this figured out. You're working for Mrs. Grimes. Checking out rumors of a relationship between Nick Grimes and Mrs. Justice?"

Jimmie looked at me shrewdly. He was a poker player. I hoped I was maintaining an adequate poker face, but I doubted it.

"Any truth to those rumors?"

"Nope. Just two people who think the same way."

"So, you are working for Mrs. Grimes?"

"Maybe. Maybe I just like a good rumor."

I knew I had to be careful with what I told Jimmie Flambeau.

"Just 'cause you're curious, huh?"

"Nosy, some people say."

He laughed, something that Jimmie Flambeau was not prone to do.

"Now, Nick Grimes is a man I'd like to know more about."

"I take it you do business with him."

"Sometimes."

I thought about it. It wouldn't be a bad thing to have Jimmie Flambeau owe you a favor, even a small one.

"Is this where we swap information?"

"What do you have to swap?"

"I know Grimes owns a place in Lewes, Delaware. Got a girl named Bonnie Blank stashed up there."

Flambeau chewed on the temple of his sunglasses while he studied me.

"Hey, that's very helpful."

"It's a small county. What goes around comes around."

"Sure," he said.

He nodded agreeably.

"Tarry Justice doesn't owe me any money, if he's still alive, which I very much doubt."

Responding to a signal not apparent to me, Felipe materialized beside me.

"I enjoyed talking to you, Mr. Proctor. Hey, see about getting yourself back to church."

Felipe tugged my sleeve. I shook him off but followed him dutifully back to my car. Ten minutes later, I was back in my office.

I'd had a good afternoon. I'd gotten a bit of information from Flambeau and gained an added benefit—a small favor owed that I could keep in my back pocket.

Jimmie Flambeau had a long memory and this insight made me search mine again.

Lincoln Charlestraton. He was the man accused of selling cocaine to Tarry Justice. I knew I'd met him before and now I remembered where.

Chapter Nine

The Missing Linc

I went straight upstairs to DP's domain. He was at his desk reading the *Post*, and I took the chair across from him.

"What do we know about Lincoln Charlestraton?"

DP folded the paper, tossed it on the floor, and closed his eyes to access his memory. "Thirty years old, single, native of Dayton Ohio, Virginia Tech grad."

He checked off the facts on his fingers, as if he'd just viewed a spreadsheet on his computer.

"He's an architect with a small firm in Old Town that does pretty high-end residential stuff."

"Where does he work?"

The notes from Charlestraton's arrest were still on DP's desk. He dug through the pile of loose papers and shuffled through them to find the arrest warrant, which he put on top so we could both read it. Charlestraton's home address was there, and we found his business address in the officer's notes. They were within walking distance of each other, along the bike path just south of the marina on Daingerfield Island where I kept my boat.

Lincoln Charlestraton.

I nodded. He had a boat on F dock, just down from mine. I'd met him while investigating the death of the man who owned the *Southern Patriot* before I did. DP wasn't the only one with a functioning memory.

The notes showed that Charlestraton had been arrested and charged with two related offenses in connection with what happened at Bomba's Beach Shack on New Year's Day.

I gestured toward DP's computer.

"Can you pull up the DC Superior Court docket sheet on this guy?"

"Sure."

It didn't take long to pull up *United States v. Charlestraton*, and to page through it. Charlestraton was out on bond. A court appointed lawyer, a Fifth Streeter, as they're known around here, had entered an appearance on his behalf on the day he was arrested. The case was set for trial in late September. Other than that, nothing. No motions, no filings, no quibbling with the prosecutor's office about details of the charge. This was a slow guilty plea in the making. I thanked DP, went to the parking lot and got in my car.

It was four o'clock. The afternoon's heat had broken, and a breeze had come up, providing northern Virginia with one of the few things rarer than an honest politician: a comfortable afternoon in late June.

I drove down the Parkway to Daingerfield Island and found a space in the marina parking lot. It would be a short and pleasant walk down the bike path to Charlestraton's business address, but I followed an impulse and opened the gate to F dock and made my way down the gray, HardiePlank dock that ran between two rows of small sailboats. My little sloop was three-quarters of the way down on the right. My lack of care was starting to show. The hull was dingy, the teak rub-rails had lost their varnished luster and the brightwork was beginning to dull. She looked as worn and tired as I felt. Seeing her now recharged the sense of guilt and remorse that had never been far from my mind since that May evening when I'd last stepped off her.

Track Racker had been an evil man and a predator. I'd always known that. But he was also a double murderer who was about to escape punishment. Well, he hadn't, but the price to be paid for exacting justice—if you could call it that—was enormous. I was left to wrestle with the consequences of personal vengeance and the price of redemption, issues I might never resolve.

I adjusted the docking lines and tightened the halyards, wondering if I'd ever steel myself to sail her again.

Charlestraton's well-maintained little sloop was in a slip a little farther down on the opposite side of the dock. As I approached, I saw something taped to the stanchion at the head of his slip—a brittle, black plastic sign with a phone number written in the white box below the red letters, spelling "For Sale." I remembered the painstaking care Charlestraton was lavishing on his boat on the day I'd met him. For some reason, the words filled me with sadness.

The Mount Vernon Trail runs north to south, connecting Alexandria and Arlington with our first president's home, seventeen miles below Alexandria. The well-maintained asphalt path winds along past Daingerfield Island through a marsh and a gently rolling margin of land between the river and the Parkway. The marsh and grass on both sides of the path were lush with midsummer green, and the cyclists were out in small pelotons, competing for space with dog walkers, roller bladers, and joggers, creating a kaleidoscopic chaos of color on the narrow path.

I walked south, keeping to the grassy fringe of the path, pondering how to get Lincoln Charlestraton to tell me what I wanted to know. I decided to trust my instincts, which is what I usually did, although not always with the best results.

Charlestraton's office was in Old Town proper, but he lived on the fourth floor of a new, brick condominium located right on the river just north of the city. Some people just can't get away from the water. Assuming he'd be at work, I stopped by his condo first, hoping to get a feel for him.

The building was secured by a four-button security pad at the entranceway door. I got the combination by loitering on the sidewalk, seemingly engrossed in my cell phone, until a careless tenant allowed me to watch her input the numbers. As soon as she got on the elevator, I let myself in. The lobby was quiet, air conditioned, and refreshingly cool. Just past the bank of elevators, a man was using a key to access his mailbox. I recognized him, even without DP's description. A slim African American of medium height, he wore an open-necked Hawaiian shirt and a pair of badly wrinkled blue Bermuda shorts.

Lincoln Charlestraton.

"Hello Linc."

He turned abruptly. He was quick, agile and edgy.

"Do I know you?"

Gone was the neat beard he had during our first encounter. I wondered if he'd shaved it for court. In its place was several days of stubble.

"You might not remember me. I met you back in May on F Dock when I was investigating Jake Carter's death."

He looked me over.

"Sure, you're Victor Lazlo."

I burst out laughing.

"I did tell you that, didn't I?"

His brow furrowed.

"That's not your name?"

"No, it's not. It's Joth Proctor."

I opened my wallet and showed him my bar card. He tilted his head and regarded me with an expression of curiosity. His unkempt appearance and midday presence at home made me wonder if the arrest had cost him his job.

"Yeah, you were involved in that double murder in Arlington last spring. What are you doing here?"

"Seeing if I can help you."

With an impulsive gesture, he shoved his hands deeply into the pockets of his shorts. "And how are you gonna do that?"

"Is there some place we can talk?"

He glanced at the door, probably wondering how I'd gotten in.

"Talk about what?"

"About what happened at Bomba's on New Year's Day."

His face took on a sour expression.

"Why do you care about that?"

"Because I represent the wife of the guy who fell off the boat that night."

He started to turn away, but I took a cautious step toward him.

"Linc, you know me. I was a friend of Jake's, and I helped his family after he was killed. That's all I'm trying to do now. Help somebody's family."

"I can't do anything about that."

"I just want to know if he's dead, and if he is, it doesn't matter how he died. He was never seen again after he left Bomba's that night and the police are listing him as missing. That kind of leaves the wife up a tree. She's just trying to get on with her life and she needs to know. If he is dead, I don't care what killed him, or who."

"I'm not talking about that. Not to her lawyer."

"What if I was your lawyer?"

He shoved his hands back into his shorts. I remembered how neat and put together he'd been when I'd met him in May. Now, he seemed ground down and tired.

"How does that work?"

"You're facing a prosecution in DC with possible jail time on the back end. You've got some Fifth Streeter representing you who will do nothing for you until the trial date, and then convince you to plead guilty. That means you'll go to jail. You realize that, don't you?"

He didn't say anything, but I could see that someone had already had that talk with him.

"I can do better than that, Linc."

"How? They found the coke in my car."

Now, I understood how a guy his age could afford a yacht and a condo on the river.

I nodded.

"There are lots of potential defenses in a case like this: chain of custody on the evidence, illegal search and seizure, validity of the testing . . . and DC police can be sloppy about the details. Is it worth talking about?"

It wasn't a topic he wanted to discuss, but I could see him weighing my request like a man with little to lose. He gulped some air.

"Okay. Let's go upstairs."

He lived in a comfortable two-bedroom condo with a great view of the Potomac and the Maryland shore. Sailboats plied the channel and the ferry that connected Old Town to the gambling mecca on the Maryland shore churned the blue water. Remembering the "For Sale" sign on his sloop, I wondered if he was having trouble carrying what must be a steep mortgage under the weight of the financial burdens of a criminal defense.

I walked over to the window to marshal my thoughts while he stepped into the kitchen. "Something to drink?"

"Bottle of water?"

He emerged with two and gestured to a leather armchair beside a gas fireplace. As he took a seat on the couch, I glanced around. His place was comfortably furnished in a clean, modern design. The furniture looked new and wall hangings showed a refined taste for expressionism.

"How long have you lived here?"

"Long enough. Tell me how you're going to help me."

I took a bottle from him and sat down.

"I'm going to continue to represent Mrs. Justice. I can represent both of you because there's no conflict. If I can have her husband declared dead, she becomes a widow, entitled to a widow's benefits. That's all I care about for her."

He processed this and nodded.

"Tarry Justice. Tall, thin guy with a sandy mustache."

"That's him."

He nodded again.

"He was there."

"I understand some people were doing cocaine that afternoon."

"It wasn't for profit, you know. I just wanted to keep the party going."

"It doesn't matter to me how he got the coke or even if he got the coke from you."

"Before we go there, what are you going to do for me?"

I folded my hands and met his eyes.

"I'll enter an appearance in the case, and you can have the pleasure of firing that Fifth Streeter. I'll do the legwork and file every legitimate motion I can come up with. We'll fight them on everything, and then we'll see if we can get the case dismissed before trial."

"And if we can't?"

"If not, I'll try the hell out of it. You're going to get a green prosecutor on a case like this. And that person is gonna run into a buzz saw at trial."

He licked his lips.

"It's not a matter of money," he said. "I've got plenty of money."

I knew that meant he didn't. It also meant that he was ready to sign on.

"Look, I'm not real busy right now. I'll need a five-thousand-dollar retainer, and I'll bill you monthly beyond that."

"What's your rate?"

I thought quickly.

"For you? Two hundred an hour."

He was thinking just as fast.

"What if I give you my boat?"

"I've already got a boat, Linc."

"What if I get behind?"

"Don't. But if you do, I'll stick with you, and you pay me when you can. If you help me."

He looked at me carefully for a long moment, then went to a sideboard near the kitchen and opened the top drawer to remove a checkbook.

"Victor Lazlo?"

"Victor Lazlo's a character from a Bogart movie."

"I know."

We shared a laugh and that cut the tension nicely.

"Jonathan Proctor."

I handed him a business card and he filled out the check. After signing it, he tore it out and handed it to me.

"Do me a favor, Joth. Don't deposit it until Monday."

I agreed.

"Okay, what do you want to know?"

I walked over to the fireplace and leaned against the mantle.

"Let's go back to New Year's Day. It was just getting dark when Justice left the party on Nick Grimes's power boat, just the two of them. A lot of people think Justice fell off the boat on the way back to the marina. It was cold. Anybody thinking right would probably have tried to stay out of the wind. But he might have been careless if he'd been partying."

"He was partying alright. We all were. It was New Year's Day. Most people there were pretty fired up."

"Do you know how much he had to drink?"

"I don't know him that well. I know his partner, Nick Grimes. Justice is a little bit of a stick in the mud, if you want to know the truth. William and Mary guy, you know?"

"They're both William and Mary guys."

"Yeah, and I know they run a bank together and they're pretty good at it. From what Nick told me, Justice is kind of the backroom work horse. Good with numbers, that sort of thing."

"What about Grimes?"

"He's a big personality, right? I assume he's the guy who brings in the business."

"But they were both pretty fired up."

He scratched his chin.

"Don't forget, I was too, but I've had a lot of reason to revisit that night over the past six months. The reason I remember Justice is because he was usually a real quiet guy. You know, the kind of guy who makes you nervous at a party? But not that day. Nick finally got him to let his hair down. So, if you were asking if he was drunk enough to fall off a boat, the answer is yes."

"The coke . . . I heard he bought . . ."

I paused and recalibrated my words.

"I heard he bought a gram from someone."

"No. That's not true."

He shook his head forcefully.

"I sold a gram to Nick. Nothing unusual about that. Tarry stayed away from that stuff."

"But Grimes shared it with him."

He scratched his chin and considered.

"No, I don't think that's likely."

I could see him thinking back.

"Coke fires you up. Justice was drunk as a zombie. He was messed up, but it wasn't from coke. But that's all I can tell you about Tarry Justice."

It took me a moment to process this. If Linc recalled the events correctly, Grimes had made a false statement to the police.

"Did you ever see Justice outside of these snowbird events?"

"Snow *man*. No. Tarry was part of the group, but he was a reluctant snowman."

"Reluctant?"

He shrugged.

"Yeah. He really didn't participate much. This New Year's thing was a tradition and I think he was trying to keep their partnership alive."

"You said it was a good partnership."

"No, I said it was a successful partnership."

He shrugged.

"It was like a bad marriage. You know, if they were making money, they had to find ways to keep it together."

So, Justice had two bad marriages. A real one and a business marriage. I felt even sorrier for him.

"Did you see him get on the boat when he and Grimes left?"

"No. I was elsewhere at that point."

"I see. Okay, let's talk about the arrest. Where'd they find the coke?"

"In the glove box in my car."

"What made them look there?"

"I don't know. When the police show, people get nervous. Somebody talked. Maybe Bomba. He knew where it was."

My ears perked up.

"They didn't have search warrant?"

"No."

"Did they ask for permission to search your car?"

"Yeah, and I said no. They did it anyway. They said they didn't need one because the car was mobile. They said they needed to search it before I had a chance to drive away with any evidence."

I knew possible contraband in an automobile could be justification for a warrantless search, depending on the facts, but the constitutional presumption made this a disfavored tactic.

"They read you your rights?"

He shook his head vigorously.

"Nope. They just said they had to do the search and they went at it."

I nodded. Every decent criminal lawyer knows that so-called exigent circumstances can provide an exception to Fourth Amendment protections against warrantless searches. And every good lawyer realizes that cops play fast and loose with the rules governing this exception.

"Since a car is mobile, sometimes a warrantless search is permitted to keep the evidence from disappearing. But there must be pretty strong justification for skipping over the usual legal protections a person is entitled to under the Constitution. There has to be something that makes the usual procedures unworkable."

"It doesn't matter. I couldn't have driven away if I wanted to."

"Why not?"

"Because Bomba had my keys."

"Bomba had your keys? How come?"

"Say what you want about Bomba, but he doesn't let people drink and drive."

"This has happened before?"

"Yeah."

He looked at his fingernails.

"I've had a couple of incidents at his place where maybe I drank a little too much. So, when I've had a couple, he asks for my keys. I don't mind. I know he's trying to keep me alive and out of jail."

"And when the cops arrived on New Year's Day, you didn't have your car keys?"

"That's what I just said."

"So, you couldn't have driven away if you wanted to?"

"Not unless Bomba gave me my keys."

"How did the cops get in?"

"I don't know. I guess Bomba gave them up. He doesn't like doing anything to create controversy with the men in blue."

I let this sit for a minute. I still had Linc's check and waved it at him.

"You know Linc, this is going to be the most well-spent five thousand dollars of your life."

Friend of the Court

***

It was nearly six o'clock when I got back to the office. I walked across to Ireland's Four Courts, a dim saloon that catered to hard drinkers, woman chasers, and the Premier League soccer crowd. I found a seat at the end of the crowded bar. Phyliss, a fresh-faced, athletic blonde who liked to get to know her customers, was on duty. She brought me bourbon on the rocks without being asked. I thanked her, and as I tasted it, I realized it was the first drink I'd had since Melanie Freeman called me out for day-drinking during office hours.

I pushed the drink away, paid for it and left. I was too busy to be drinking and I liked it that way.

Chapter Ten

Grave Matters

I didn't sleep well that night, haunted by the image of an imposing, ghostly figure in Confederate gray. A steady rain began at midnight and tapered off at dawn. When I got up, the leaves of the magnolia in my yard were dripping and fog rose from the grass. It felt like a good morning to fulfill a duty I'd been putting off for too long. I got in my car and drove to the St. James Catholic Cemetery in the city of Falls Church.

The cemetery, which dates back to the Civil War, occupies a gently sloping plot of land off a busy road. It's enclosed by a stone wall and gated like an Old-World citadel. The gate was locked, but the wall was not high enough to keep out a spry 37-year-old. I took a quick look around and vaulted over it.

It was easy to spot a fresh grave amid uneven rows of the kind of grim, ornate, and gothic markers that had been favored in earlier times. Over a plot in the corner, away from the road, a polished granite headstone read "Jennifer J. Tedesco" above the dates of her birth and death—dates with too few years between them.

I had anticipated this moment many times, but dreaded it too much to have composed an elegy or even organized any coherent thoughts. I listened to the boisterous voices of a pair of wrens in an oak and squirrels gamboling playfully on the unmowed grass.

Once again, I tried to grasp the inequity of a higher power that would allow a valuable and promising life to be so wantonly snuffed out. I was roused from my reverie by the sound of a twig snapping. A familiar figure in a roman collar emerged from the mist and strode forward. It was Father John Tedesco, wearing a long gray raincoat and a gray face.

Blessed is he who comes in the name of the Lord.

Those dusty words, formed involuntarily in my mind, conjured baroque images of atonement, redemption, and judgment. I took a deep breath.

"Did you jump the wall, Father?"

He let his head wag and laughed.

"No."

He held something up and the emerging sun glinted off the silver metal.

"I've got a key. I can get you one."

My eyes shifted to the polished granite.

"That won't be necessary."

Having keys to a graveyard sounded like bad mojo to me. I'd rather jump the wall.

He assumed the spot at the opposite side of Jenny's grave. We both studied the marker as if an answer was contained in the inscription. He rocked on his heels and glanced at me.

"I thought I might run into you here someday."

"To tell the truth, it's my first visit. I'm a little ashamed to admit it."

He nodded gravely.

"The death of a loved one is always hard because we are left behind to pick up and mend the broken pieces."

Death—and life—was his métier; it was not hard for him to dredge up the simple and reassuring cliche. But I suspected he knew that it was even more than that to me.

"Any death can be a hard thing," I said. "How often do you make it down here?"

"Almost every morning. I come down after Mass."

He gave me a tired smile and turned his hands up.

"You see, I'm a priest. She's the only family I have. Or will have."

I remembered what Melanie had said and shared it with him.

"You've got your church, your family, you call it. Where I grew up, the priests talked about the parish as their flock."

"You're right," he said, and laughed. "It's my family. And more so now than ever. It's a good way to think of it. A group to be nurtured and defended."

He was a melodramatic man, prone to the theatrical gesture and the overcooked phrase. An awkward pause followed, and I filled it.

"You know, she was all I had, too."

He looked me over and seemed to recalibrate.

"No siblings?"

I thought again of my long-dead brother. The anger and distrust of the Catholic hierarchy had dissipated with the years but had never been erased.

"No."

"Well, things can still change for you. You're still young enough."

"Maybe."

I shifted my feet, wondering if he was speculating about Melanie and me. I realized that what he thought mattered to me.

I looked again at Jenny's gravestone.

"Do you think we can do any good?"

"For her? I know what the church teaches. But we come here for ourselves, Joth."

More Catholic guilt, but this was coming at me in a new form.

"Is it wrong to try and find some peace with it?"

"I'd like to find some peace, too. I'd like to know who killed her."

This acknowledgement of a worldly motive struck me as a significant admission.

"I see. And, then what?"

"I'd feel the need to forgive him."

"To make you feel better or him?"

"Then, it was a man?"

"It was a man."

"I'd like to know what happened to her."

"You know the answer to that. She was poisoned."

He saw something in my expression.

"It wasn't a suicide?"

A change in his voice revealed a subtle anxiety. This was a theological matter with which I was familiar. The Catholic church relies on its elaborate ceremonies and rituals to provide comfort and thereby own your psyche. It also presents a panoply of absolute and often draconian doctrines. I realized he believed that suicide would condemn his sister to eternal damnation, and he cared about that.

"Of course not."

"That's not what the police say."

He was sweating, and I could see that my answer might provide great relief to him.

"Someone gave her poison, Father. You know that."

"Not necessarily. But I don't want to obsess over it."

"That's easy. You can stop believing in fairy tales."

"Once we do that, where do we stop? Do we discount everything not subject to empirical proof?"

"Yes."

"A poisoned apple."

He was struggling to find a way to frame the question.

"But how? Why?"

"The poison was meant for someone else."

"Why haven't the authorities prosecuted? Is it because she was an ecdysiast?"

"A stripper, you mean?"

"She was my sister. It would help if I knew what happened to her."

"I'll tell you when I can, Father."

"I'd like to think that there's some justice."

He's as conflicted as I am.

"I thought you just wanted to forgive him?"

"Justice would help."

What about justice? Track had killed two people and would have gotten away with it.

"Justice is hard to come by in this world. But you're a priest. You can be confident of what happens in the next one."

"She wasn't a bad girl. That is a great source of con-solation."

"Not for me," I said.

"Then, you are left to fight it out with yourself here on Earth."

"I know. But that's what we're all doing, isn't it? Trying to fight it out?"

"What we need to do, I think, is get to a place where we don't have to fight anymore."

"Let me know when you get there," I said.

He was used to being challenged and was prepared to respond.

"And where are you trying to get?"

I looked up and met his eyes. He was a priest, and I was a Catholic, or had been. He held in his small, uncal-loused hands the thing I needed—absolution—and I only had to do two things to get it. Ask for it and believe in it. I wouldn't do the first and couldn't do the second. It wasn't like Tinkerbell; you couldn't just say you be-lieved and talk yourself into it. And to ask for it would be to confess to him, and thereby put myself into those little hands.

I looked again at her grave.

"I just want to find the right words to say. The right thoughts to think."

He appeared unsurprised and untroubled by this admission.

"Don't overthink it, Joth. Just put in the time. It will come to you."

"What will come to me?"

"I don't know. But you will."

He nodded and turned to go. I watched his slow, steady strides as he departed.

People sometimes ask cheerfully how I avoided the Massachusetts college of my ancestors; why I left Salem. I tell them I was offered a lacrosse scholarship. That was not untrue. I went to college to play lacrosse, but I came south because I needed to find a new life, and I did, but I ended up replacing the ghosts that had bedeviled my family since 1692 with new ones of my own making.

***

By the time I got back to work, the summer sun had evaporated the mist and the grass was drying out. As I got into the office, I immediately noticed that someone had rearranged the clutter I had left on top of my desk. In a cleared space in the center of this debris, a large yellow post-it note had been affixed to the leather surface.

The word "DOUBLEDAY" appeared on the note in DP's recognizable block print. I carefully considered it before putting the paper in my pocket.

I went out to the parking lot and got back into my car.

Arlington National Cemetery is a ten-minute drive from my office; long enough to assure myself that I was not being followed. I parked in the visitor's center, then trudged past John Kennedy's eternal flame and up the long rise to the Custis-Lee Mansion and the most breathtaking vista in Arlington.

Against the majestic backdrop of the capitol's monuments and memorials and the winding Potomac River, I looked down on acres of rolling hills, emerald grass, and uniform ranks of simple marble headstones, gleaming in the summer sun.

In 1863, the United States government foreclosed on the mansion and the extensive property surrounding it. The owner at the time, a certain Robert Edward Lee, had failed to pay his taxes. The federal government turned Arlington House and its property into the final resting place for many of Lee's most bitter opponents, including many high-ranking Union generals.

A few hundred yards behind the mansion is a granite obelisk, marked "DOUBLEDAY" in tarnished brass letters. Abner Doubleday didn't invent baseball, but he commanded the Union First Corps for several critical hours at the battle of Gettysburg.

DP sat with his eyes closed, the sun on his face, and his back rested against Doubleday's gravestone. He bounced nimbly to his feet as he heard me approach.

"This must be important."

"It might be. I'm just being careful."

He held out a thin legal document.

"I got served with this yesterday afternoon."

It was a warrant allowing the Arlington police to search DP's office for "all evidence documenting or bearing on discussions with Jonathan Proctor, Esquire, regarding Frank 'Track' Racker or his disappearance."

This didn't shock me, but it took a moment to process.

"They talk to you?"

"A little bit."

He shrugged.

"I didn't have much to tell them. I didn't open a file and I don't have any records. I remember talking to you about him a little bit, but just general things. I don't remember what was said."

I did. I had asked him where a client of mine might obtain arsenic. I hadn't tied the inquiry to Track, but DP knew how to put two and two together.

"So, you had nothing for them?"

"Nope."

I looked again through the papers.

"Why all the secrecy?"

"Did you get one of these?"

"No, although I'm sure it's coming."

"Maybe not."

I looked at him and tried to follow his thinking.

"Maybe you're just a shot in the dark; somebody's hunch?"

"That's not how I figure it."

I gave up.

"Okay."

"What would they expect me to do once I got the warrant? Either call you or walk downstairs to talk to you. Maybe say things that wouldn't be in any records that a search would turn up. Stuff that might be a problem."

DP looked at me without flinching. He knew what had happened to Track. He'd figured it out within days of when it happened. That's what DP did; he put pieces together from faint hints and clues; from a gesture, a slant of the eyebrow, a word unsaid.

He knows, but my secret is safe with him.

I ran a hand back through my unkempt hair.

"Right."

It was starting to make sense.

"Phones and the office? Both?"

"Probably."

"Can you run a scan?"

"It'll take me a couple of days to get the equipment."

I gave the warrant back to him.

"Alright. That's good to know."

"If that's their play, Joth, then it's good news."

"And how is having your office bugged good news?"

"It means they got nothing. They're grasping at straws."

I remembered the look of gleeful malice I had seen on Detective Anderson's face at the sports pub, but he wasn't the one calling the shots. DP let me process his insight and it began to make sense, this long shot ploy.

"I hope Heather thinks that."

"You know what? You need to stop worrying about what Heather thinks."

DP was the only person with an insight into how important Heather's opinion was to me; not even Irish Dan knew that.

"You're right. But that's what I hope, just the same."

I took a lungful of air.

"Anything else?"

"No."

He closed with his usual end note.

"I'll snoop around."

I told him I appreciated it and we left the cemetery by separate routes. On my way out, I took a short detour into the oldest section of the cemetery, where I laid my hand on the cold marble of a headstone that read:

COLONEL NATHANIEL H. PROCTOR
20TH MASSACHUSETTS VOLUNTEERS
KIA GETTYSBURG

Chapter Eleven

Making Law

It was now July, the middle of another stifling DC summer, and Tarry Justice had been missing for more than the statutorily mandated six months. Justice was as dead as my great-great-grandfather, and although questions remained about how and why, there didn't seem to be much doubt about the principal fact.

I sat down in front of my computer, pulled up the notes of my discussions with Bobbitt and Liz and opened the Virginia Code to the presumption of death statute. Over the course of a few fast-moving hours, I drafted a bare-bones Complaint for Declaratory Judgment, asking the Arlington Circuit Court to declare as a fact this obvious truth: Tarry Justice was legally dead, and Bobbitt was a widow. Under the statute, I needed to prove only three elements to win my case: that Justice hadn't been seen in six months; that he'd been last seen on a boat underway in the Potomac River, and that the Potomac fell within the Virginia legislature's idea of the "high seas."

The first two prongs were so straightforward that I didn't expect any real argument from the Commonwealth, but there was very little case law interpreting "high seas" and none in this context. This meant that the judge would not be constrained by unfavorable precedent and would have broad latitude to do what he or she wanted or thought the facts and law demanded. While the Potomac hardly sounded like anyone's idea of the high seas, this was a legal construct and not a phrase circumscribed by conventional understanding.

Any court's ultimate job is to do justice and since we could show that Bobbitt's husband was undoubtedly dead, I believed the judge might be persuaded to stretch a legal point to get a fair result. The only real question was the level of push back I could expect to get from the Commonwealth Attorney's office. I reread the Complaint several times and had Marie spell check and format it. Then, I walked it over to the Clerk of the Court's office and filed it.

Since the respondent was the Commonwealth of Virginia, the suit would be served on the Secretary of the Commonwealth in Richmond. In due course, under the statutory process, the Complaint would find its way back to the Commonwealth's Attorney in the filing jurisdiction. That would be my old friend and occasional adversary, Heather Burke, a woman who knew me as well as anyone.

The problem for Heather and me was that our relationship had started out too hot. Not too hot sexually, although that was certainly true, but too hot emotionally. By the end of a handful of whirlwind days, we had declared our love for each other and that had been a mistake, at least for Heather. We set too high a standard for ourselves and when the challenges inevitably developed, we butted up against a commitment we impetuously made with no place to retreat. Heather found herself like the winning bidder at an auction, desperately trying to retract her bid, with me playing the role of the befuddled auctioneer. We were long past that now, and for Heather our romance was as faded as an old valentine, tucked in a book and discovered decades later.

When she called me three days later, she sounded angry.

"What's this all about?"

I could hear her shaking the Complaint in her hand. While Heather could be testy and impatient, her reaction startled me.

"What's *what* all about?"

"*in re Tarrant Justice.* You want a declaration of death because a guy fell off a boat?"

"That was six months ago and in the dead of winter. He's dead, and everybody knows it. The poor woman needs to get on with her life."

"Excuse me for sounding cynical. Anytime someone disappears under unusual circumstances, my ears prick up. Especially if you're involved."

She employed that dagger with a twist that hurt.

"What are you implying?"

"Your client had a motive and there's nothing implied about it."

"My client wasn't on the boat."

I thought about what Liz Hillman had told me.

"Besides, as far as I know, they had a happy marriage."

"As far as you know."

I cringed and tried to walk the qualifier back.

"That's right. But the status of their marriage is not my business."

"I happen to know they lived separate lives."

"How do you happen to know that?" I said, "unless you have some stake in this."

"I have a stake in seeing that justice is done."

"The law puts the Potomac River in DC. He drowned outside your jurisdiction. If you want to do justice, help this woman get past it."

"So, it's about money?"

"It's about settling his estate, yes. It's unfair to reduce that to money."

"Isn't that what it is?"

The discussion seemed pointless, and she was wearing me down.

"It's part of it, sure. But this isn't a divorce. She can't claim his assets or probate the will until the court declares him dead."

Something about that comment sparked her curiosity.

"They have a prenup?"

"A prenuptial agreement? What are you talking about?"

She pounced.

"Here's how I see it. Justice was a wealthy man and he had kids from his first marriage. Not the kind of guy to marry a middle-aged gold digger without a prenup."

"Are you stating facts or asking me a question?"

She ignored me.

"The idea of a prenup is to keep a wealthy husband's money intact in case he married a bimbo who was only in it for the cash. If there's a prenup, she can't divorce him without losing her claim on his assets. But if he dies, that's different. That's usually how a prenup works."

"I don't know anything about that."

"Well, you better find out."

"What do you care, anyway?"

It was a foolish question. Heather had a rare ability to sustain her anger.

"Nobody's found a body. We don't know what happened to Justice, do we?"

"This isn't a criminal case," I said. "He's disappeared and he's not coming back. He's dead, Heather."

"Justice had money. If she divorced him, depending on what a prenup says, she could be rich or just another middle-aged hussy, trying to make ends meet."

I took in a lungful of air for her benefit.

"That's quite a statement, considering you don't know what you're talking about."

I heard her slam something down.

"I'm going to send you a Request for Production of Documents. If she's got a prenup, I want it."

"And I've got a question for you. Do Tarry Justice's kids live in the county?"

"What's that got to do with anything?"

"Let me ask it this way. They wouldn't be friends of yours, would they?"

"I want that prenup," she said, and slammed down the receiver.

As I hung up, I wondered if there was anyone out there recording the conversation. If so, at least they'd finally heard something to snap the hour-by-hour boredom that constituted my current professional life. I also concluded that if my phone lines were tapped, Heather must not know about it. She'd have been much more circumspect in her language if she thought it would go beyond the two of us.

***

It seemed as if her Request for Production of Documents was in my inbox by the time I hung up the phone. I printed it out and looked it over while nursing a cup of stale coffee. The request covered only one category of documents: "Produce any and all pre- or post-nuptial contracts, agreements or other arrangements limiting or conditioning Rachel Justice's interest or claim to Tarry Justice's assets or estate upon divorce or other termination of their marriage."

Not to be outdone, I sent my objections back that afternoon. Nothing that she wanted had any legal relevance to the question before the court, and I wanted the satisfaction of having a judge deny her request.

I called her office and asked for her longtime secretary, Betty. She provided Heather's available hearing dates and I called the clerk's office to set our discovery dispute for the first one available: Friday of the following week.

I slept even less well than usual that night, chewing on the double stress of DP's subpoena and Heather's edgy rebuke. She was right about one thing; a prenup would explain a lot. I remembered Bobbitt mentioning that she'd signed a contract obligating her to change her last name as a condition of marrying Justice. What other terms did that contract contain?

By dawn, I'd reframed it as a question of what Liz Hillman knew and what she was holding back. Maybe this was why she dumped the case on me—as subtle revenge for dumping her. I'd be damned before I'd let her play me for a sap.

I got her on the phone just after lunch. She filled me in with unwanted small talk about old friends that remained in her circle and the newest guy she was dating. Then, I worked her around to the point of my call.

"Did they have a prenup? Justice and Bobbitt?"

She was a cagey lawyer.

"A prenup?"

"She wasn't seeking a divorce when she came to see you, but she presented a case that would get her around a typical prenup."

"So?"

"So, let's assume they had one. Wouldn't that probably provide that she's disqualified from the bulk of his money if she divorces him, but not if he dies?"

"Didn't you take domestic relations in law school?"

"Yeah, but only to meet pretty girls."

"You could ask your client. Or maybe not."

"You're not going to tell me, are you?"

She paused, then took her time with her last point.

"There are some things you are better off not knowing, Joth."

I hung up the phone and considered what she'd said. Maybe she was right. I usually got myself in hot water when I went tilting at windmills.

Just do your job.

But if I put aside the quest for justice, I'd have a job, but no purpose. And, without a purpose, I'd wallow in guilt and misery.

Chapter Twelve

Round One with Heather

DP dropped by the next afternoon. He had a smile on his face and a bounce in his step.

"That thing we talked about?"

He nodded toward the phone.

"The answer is yes."

"I see. You want to walk over to the courthouse?"

"Sure."

Instead, we walked in the opposite direction and ducked into the lobby of a Wilson Boulevard office building.

"Bugged?"

"Yeah, and not just the phones."

I was not surprised, but it was still a hard truth to accept.

"But you can block it?"

"There's a couple of things we can do. Disable it, or just pump some white noise into it. That way, they won't be sure you discovered it. They might just think it broke down. They might try to fix it."

"No, I want them to know. What are they going to do, complain? It doesn't do them much good to bug my office if I'm aware of it."

"True enough."

"Use your imagination. That's what you're good at."

***

The Circuit Court occupies the fifth floor of the Arlington Courthouse, and there are only four courtrooms, matching the number of circuit court judges in this historically sleepy jurisdiction. Each courtroom features high ceilings and dark wood paneling. Technological marvels when the courthouse opened in the 1990s, they remained up to date with the latest audio-visual equipment, none of which would be needed for my sparring contest with Heather.

Friday morning was Motion's Day in Arlington, a chance for the court to rule on procedural disputes that could be decided without evidence in a half an hour or less. Whether Heather got the documents she'd requested, and whether I'd even ask Bobbitt if she had a prenup, would depend not on facts, but on the court's determination of the legal relevance of Heather's request.

Heather arrived dressed to kill in a blood red pant suit, the color she reserved to signal moral outrage. She wore her strawberry blonde hair pulled back, giving her a stripped down for action look. After the sort of curt good mornings that boxers sometimes exchange when entering the ring, Heather and I found seats in opposite corners on the public benches outside the courtroom, where we waited for the court to process the uncontested matters and for our case to work its way to the top of the pile.

The nine o'clock docket was thin, and it was not yet ten when the bailiff stepped outside and called *in re Tarrant Justice*. I held the door for her and followed her in. She strode in without acknowledging my gesture. But that's all it was, a gesture. I was there to win.

The presiding judge was Anne Gabriel. A former state delegate who had never tried a case. She'd been foisted on the bench by unhappy colleagues in the legislature who found her imperious and incurious and apparently thought the bench was the perfect place to exile her. Gabriel had been raised in Arlington and had been a year ahead of Heather in law school. Even her detractors, and there were many, acknowledged that she was smart and ambitious. Even with the backward step her appointment to the bench might have seemed, she'd come a long way in a short time.

Heather and I moved up inside the bar, taking our places at the counsel tables positioned on either side of the podium. Gabriel glanced at the docket sheet. I guessed she hadn't read either of our briefs, but she had shrewd piercing eyes behind horn rim glasses, eyes that probed the two lawyers for clues and insights.

"This is your motion, Mr. Proctor?"

"Yes, your honor."

I stepped up to the podium, adjusted the microphone and after stating the argument, I concluded as succinctly as I could.

"This is about whether a man who fell off a moving boat and disappeared into the Potomac River six months ago fits the definition of lost at sea within the meaning of the statute. And that's all it's about. If he did, we think his wife is entitled to be declared what the facts make her out to be—a widow. The Commonwealth's request is irrelevant because our petition is not an excuse for a fishing expedition into the dead man's life and financial affairs."

I sat down.

Heather knew she had a more difficult argument, especially when arguing before a judge as notoriously lazy as Anne Gabriel.

"This is a novel theory, your Honor, and the Commonwealth has a duty to police the use of a curative statute to circumvent a financial agreement between husband and wife that would have been disadvantageous to the plaintiff in the case of divorce."

I loved convoluted sentences like that, as they tended to put the judge to sleep, but Gabriel surprised me. The case must have piqued her interest because she smiled and asked the question I was hoping she would ask.

"As far as the law's concerned, this case isn't even about whether he's dead, is it? It's about whether the three prongs of the statutory requirement for this relief have been fulfilled. What difference does his financial arrangement with his wife make?"

"Because she might have had a motive to commit a crime."

Gabriel leaned forward and folded her hands under her chin.

"Are you suggesting she killed her husband?"

"I'm suggesting it's not impossible."

Gabriel shook her distinguished head.

"That's quite a statement, Ms. Burke. You're going to need some evidence to support that theory before I let you go digging into their personal relationship."

That was all I needed to hear. I reshuffled my papers and waited for Heather to exhaust the judge's patience. That didn't take long. After five more minutes of recycled arguments, Gabriel brought her gavel down once.

"The objection to the Commonwealth's discovery request is sustained. Mr. Proctor, if you'll draft an order to that effect and present it to the clerk, I'll sign it."

She called the next case.

Heather did not like to lose. As we walked out of the courtroom, she snarled at me.

"You know a lot about people disappearing mysteriously, don't you?"

Normally, I would have pushed back. Instead, I answered warily.

"A lot less than you do."

It was a nice rejoinder, but it didn't take the sting out of Heather's cold rebuke.

***

I had another matter to put on another docket: a motion to suppress the evidence in *United States v. Charlestraton*, pending across the river in Washington, D.C. This was a simpler, more straightforward argument and because I'd made it a half dozen times before, I already had the necessary research in a file in my office.

Basic constitutional law makes it impermissible for the authorities—the United States in any case involving Washington, DC—to conduct a search and seizure without due process. Somebody had told the police that Charlestraton was the source of the cocaine being distributed at Bomba's on New Year's Day. The investigating cop asked Charlestraton if he could search his car and he had refused, as was his right. What the officer should have done then was impound Charlestraton's Audi until the police could obtain a lawfully issued warrant to search it. But it was New Year's Day for the arresting officer, too, and he was probably hung over and in a hurry to get home to watch the bowl games. So, he skipped a step by demanding the keys from Bomba and searching the car under the justification that cars are inherently mobile and that Charlestraton might drive off with the evidence at any time. But he couldn't—not if Bomba had the keys.

By five o'clock, I had drafted, proofed, and finalized the motion.

Unlike in Arlington, where the parties choose their court dates on preliminary matters, DC tells you when you'll be heard. I filed the Motion in the D.C. Superior Court with a copy to the U. S. Attorney's office and waited to be told when a judge would hear me.

Chapter Thirteen

Truth or Consequences

Days passed, and then a week went by with no further developments in Bobbitt's case. Heather issued no more discovery, sought no depositions, and subpoenaed no witnesses. There were none of the pre-trial motions a party usually filed when trying to limit or shape a case.

The Commonwealth appeared prepared to stand on the somewhat logical argument that the Potomac was not the high seas and that was fine with me. Other than to subpoena and prep my witnesses, and file my exhibits before trial, there was nothing else I needed to do to put my case together. The key witness, the one I worried about, would be Nicholas Grimes, the only person who could testify that Tarry Justice disappeared from a boat underway on the Potomac River.

Grimes was a difficult man to run down. He didn't respond to emails, and he replied to my phone calls by calling my office line either early in the morning or late at night, when I would not likely be there. Fortunately, I keep eccentric hours and was in my office one morning when he called at seven.

He seemed flustered to hear a live voice.

"I'm hoping to leave a message for Jonathan Proctor," he said.

"This is Joth Proctor. What can I do for you?"

It took him a moment to recover and identify himself.

"I understand you've been trying to speak to me."

"That's right. As I think you know, I represent Mrs. Justice in her effort to gain some closure in respect to her husband."

"Yes, she mentioned that to me."

"I know this is painful, but you were the last person to see him. I'd like to get your cooperation and your testimony at trial. Mrs. Justice's case depends on what you tell the judge."

"At trial? That would be difficult. As you know, with Tarry gone we're under the gun here at the bank and time away is very problematic."

"We really need your testimony. Bobbitt needs your testimony."

"Could I submit an affidavit? I'll state whatever you want."

I smiled. This was a familiar dodge by a reluctant witness.

"Unfortunately, an affidavit is not admissible at trial."

"But it would be if the Commonwealth agrees. At least that's what I've been told."

I wondered who told him that.

"That's true, but you don't know our Common-wealth's Attorney."

"I've been following this, of course. Bobbitt says that what you need me to say is that Tarry got on the boat at Bomba's and he wasn't on the boat when I got to the Pentagon marina. Is that right?"

"I'm afraid it's a little bit more complicated than that. I'd need you to fill in some of the details. The court likes to have some context."

"But these are the two facts you need to prove the case?"

"Yes," I said. "That, and that you haven't seen him since that night."

"And none of that is really in dispute."

He was trying my patience, but I maintained a cooperative tone.

"It doesn't seem to be, but you never know how it will play out at trial."

"So, it's actually pretty simple. I'll tell you what I'll do. I'll give you an affidavit attesting to the facts you need to support your position. You write it out just the way you want it and present it to me, and I'll sign it. You show it to Ms. Burke and ask if she'll accept it in lieu of my appearance at trial. She knows we've been struggling in Tarry's absence to keep the bank afloat, and as a public servant, I'm sure she'll be sympathetic to the needs of a small community business. You see if she'll accept my proposal. I think she will, but if she doesn't, I'll commit to appearing at trial."

In truth, Grimes didn't want to face possible cross-examination. Topics like how much he'd had to drink, and whether he had used cocaine could require answers that might have professional repercussions. But I didn't want that either. The last thing a trial lawyer wants is a key witness who could be subject to a withering cross examination. The second to last thing a trial lawyer wants is an uncooperative key witness. They can be cajoled into testifying truthfully, but they sometimes do so with a sour reluctance that taints the whole case.

Either way, putting Grimes on the stand didn't appeal to me, and if I could get that evidence in without taking a risk, why not? I didn't think Heather would agree to Grimes's stipulation, but I told him I'd call her. And I did.

Heather had been frosty to me for so long that I expected nothing else, but her voice on the phone sounded subdued, even cautious, and the absence of the recent venom suggested a preoccupation with bigger matters.

As I introduced the reason for the call, there was no petty chirping or gratuitous insults. She was all business.

"Look, Heather," I said, after we'd danced around it for a minute or two. "I don't want to waste the court's time proving something that's not in dispute, and it only compounds the problem if I ask Grimes to waste most of a day testifying about how his business has been hurt by his partner's disappearance."

She understood my point. I could picture her nodding.

"Undermining a prominent business isn't in my best interest either," she said.

I felt like I'd gotten lucky, and I didn't want to push my good fortune.

"I'll tell you what. Let me put together an affidavit and I'll let you look at it. Then, you can tell me what you think. If you're okay with it, I'll offer that instead of his testimony."

"That sounds reasonable. But no commitment until I see what it says."

Heather had a temper, but she didn't hold a grudge. I hung up, wondering if we'd finally worked through the issues that had developed between us since late May. If so, maybe we could recapture our long-standing relationship as each other's confidante. If not, I'd have to continue to watch my back.

***

An affidavit is something of an art form; at least I think it is. The secret is to make the critical points in the most cogent and straightforward manner possible while at the same time avoiding the sensitive matters that are the usual reasons for trying to keep the witness out of court in the first place, and without calling attention to that ploy.

It took me a couple of hours to put it together, and while Marie was putting it into final form, I called Nick Grimes. Suddenly, he wasn't so hard to reach.

"Ms. Burke has tentatively agreed to accept the affidavit in place of your personal testimony. I just finished it and I'd like to go over it with you."

"Fine. Just send it over and I'll review it. I'm sure I'll be able to sign it."

I didn't mind taking a shortcut or two, but something about Grimes's cavalier attitude toward legal formality didn't sit right. I wanted to reach a judgment about him firsthand before I offered his statement as evidence.

"No, Mr. Grimes, I think I'd like to go over it with you first. I need to satisfy myself that this is the best approach."

"It'll be very hard to find the time . . ."

"Well, find it!"

Certain people caved quickly when I lost patience. As I suspected, this self-important businessman was one of them.

"Alright. I could see you for a few minutes at perhaps 4:30?"

"That'll be fine. I see that you're in Ballston. Can you be at Saigon Breeze by then?"

"I know the place. Yes, Saigon Breeze at 4:30. I'll be there."

**

I rounded up DP and Marie and we got to Saigon Breeze by 4:15. I needed Marie in her capacity as a notary public. DP's job was to snoop. I didn't trust Nicholas Grimes and I wanted another set of eyes to assess him.

Marie and I took a four-top near the window facing the door. After a few words with his uncle, DP put on a black smock bearing the restaurant's logo and assumed the role of waiter.

Grimes was so late that I'd begun to think he wasn't going to show up, but he was easy to recognize as he walked in. He had thinning, wind-blown blond hair, and a walrus mustache over a weak chin. I took a closer look at him as he sat down. He had been a handsome man not long ago, but a web of visible veins had reddened his nose. His gold-rimmed glasses and an owl-eyed expression suggested a disheveled and disorganized prep school English teacher. He dressed like one, too, with a button-down shirt and an old-school tie with blue foulards.

I stood up and shook his hand, and he looked curiously at Marie. I introduced her and explained that she was a notary, here to attest to his signature. He stroked his chin, and I thought for a moment that he expected to escape this meeting without a formal commitment, but that wasn't going to happen. Marie had her laptop open, and it was linked to DP's uncle's printer.

"Drink?"

"Oh no, never before five."

I looked at my watch. It was ten of five and I was confident he'd be toasted by seven. I took another look at the walrus mustache and asked DP for a Vodka Collins. Marie asked for water and after a moment's consideration, Grimes did, too.

I didn't have any interest in small talk, and after his sullen agreement to fit me in, I didn't feel the need. I handed him the affidavit. He resettled his glasses on his nose and scanned it.

"Mr. Grimes, I've set out the salient points in simple and direct language."

Using my index finger as a guide, I walked him through each element of the statement. "That you and Tarry Justice boarded your motorboat the *Blue Mist* in the late morning of New Year's Day; that you traveled up the Potomac, docking at the landing that serves Bomba's Beach Shack in Georgetown; that you and Mr. Justice spent the afternoon there celebrating the holiday; that you and Justice left in the *Blue Mist* just as it was growing dark; that Mr. Justice occupied the stern while you handled the wheel; that you focused your attention on navigating the river; that you made no stops during the journey and encountered no other boats; that you heard no sound of distress from Justice; that Justice was not on the boat when you returned to the Pentagon Marina; that you've not seen or heard from Justice since. You'll see that there are a few other noncontroversial statements just to supply context."

I gave him a moment to consider the statements.

"I assume you can sign this under oath?"

He listened to me intently and then studied the affidavit thoroughly as he resumed stroking his chin.

"I'm not sure I can sign this as it is."

"Why is that?"

"Well, there are a few things that aren't quite right."

"Such as?"

"Well for one, Tarry's actual given name is not Tarry, it's Tarrant. We ought to have that set out."

I nodded at Marie. She opened the laptop and with a few strokes of her fast-moving fingers, made the requested change.

"Anything else?"

"I don't like the word, 'motorboat.' Teenagers operate motorboats. The *Blue Mist* is a Pursuit 2460 Denali with a 33 horsepower Volvo Penta V8. That's what it should say."

He took a deep breath with the ostentatious air of ownership. I nodded at Marie, who made this change as well. This went on for a few minutes, until Grimes understood that I'd gladly make all his petty changes and that his tactics would not delay the result. When he finally approved it, Marie hit the print button and I nodded to DP.

"He'll have the final to us in a moment," I said.

Then I fixed Grimes with a hard, searching look that made him readjust his glasses.

"This will be the best thing for Mrs. Justice," he said.

"Undoubtedly."

"Yes," he said. "It's been a long haul for her. Very difficult. She's suffered these last six months."

"She deserves better."

The silence that followed seemed to increase his anxiety.

"She's an elegant woman," he said.

Elegant? It was hard for me to employ that term with someone I didn't like, but if he intended it to describe a person who carried herself with an unabashed superiority in style and attitude, then perhaps he was right.

"Yes, I suppose she is. Of course, this will also allow the bank to move forward."

"That's of far less consequence to me."

"Of course."

DP brought over the revised draft. Grimes adjusted his glasses and read it carefully. He took a fountain pen out of his inside jacket pocket and signed it with a flourish. I handed it to Marie to add the notary seal.

"Would you like a copy?"

"That won't be necessary. I assume I won't be needed in court?"

"Assuming Ms. Burke is satisfied. I think she will be. I'll send you a subpoena if I need you."

He got up abruptly.

"Good day," he said, and left.

When we were sure he was gone, DP came over and took the seat Grimes had occupied. "His partner's dead and he just made it official. Not a hint of sorrow or regret. He didn't even bother to fake it."

"It's been six months," Marie said. "I'm sure he's come to grips with it."

But Marie had a trusting heart.

"Yeah, I noticed the same thing," I said to DP. "Business as usual."

"Fucking bankers," he said, shaking his head.

I smiled and nodded. Then I opened the fortune cookie that DP had puckishly delivered with Grimes' glass of water. "Justice delayed is justice denied," it read.

Chapter Fourteen

Put Up or Shut Up

Rather than passing a simple and straight-forward case to one of her assistants, Heather Burke decided to handle *in re Tarrant Justice* herself. I assumed this was because the facts of the case interested her and because it was a chance to "make law," to establish the practical impact of an untested statute.

The lost-at-sea provision in the presumption of death statute had never been thoroughly vetted in a Virginia court, and Heather wasn't above wanting to see her name in the legal journals. But after her discovery motion was denied, she seemed to lose interest. Perhaps she figured she'd taken her best shot at it or maybe she had other, more substantial cases to deal with. In any event, there were no further proceedings until the day of trial.

Because they are straight forward and urgent in nature, Declaratory Judgments are put on a fast track in Arlington. We had a hearing date in mid-August. It went to trial on a Tuesday morning in Courtroom Three, where we'd argued the discovery motion over the prenup.

Just before ten, Heather and I settled into the counsel tables. Bobbitt, dressed entirely in black in what I considered a patently insincere effort to communicate mourning, sat next to me. Heather was alone, dressed in green rather than her customary red. We'd drawn Anne Gabriel again as the presiding judge.

"All rise."

The bailiff's voice rang out as Judge Gabriel entered and assumed her seat on the high mahogany bench. She glanced down at the docket sheet the clerk had placed before her.

"This comes upon Plaintiff's request for a declaration of death?"

"That's right, your honor."

She glanced from Heather to me, and then looked appraisingly at Bobbitt. There was no jury and she was within her rights to take a less formal approach.

"Are the parties in agreement on the facts?"

Heather stood up.

"We'll stipulate to the facts, Your Honor."

"Just a minute, Your Honor," I said, rising. "There's facts and there's facts. There are some facts I'd like you to hear."

Gabriel folded her hands and looked at me with a weary disgust.

"What sort of facts, Mr. Proctor?"

"I'm ready to introduce evidence to establish the temperature of the water in the Potomac River that day."

"Stipulated," said Heather.

"And, that a drunken man of Mr. Justice's weight wouldn't have survived more than an hour-and-a-half in water that cold."

"Stipulated," said Heather.

She held up a copy of Grimes' affidavit, which we had submitted to the court in the pretrial filings.

"We'll also stipulate that he was last seen on a boat underway on the Potomac River and that he hasn't been seen or heard from in the six months since. None of that is disputed."

Judge Gabriel looked at me and waited. I concluded that Heather didn't want the judge to hear and see evidence that would put a human spin on the case. Her best chance to win was to limit the argument to the letter of the law.

Is the Potomac River the high seas?

I wanted the chance to put on the evidence because I thought it would impact the judge's willingness to stretch the law to accommodate the human challenges facing this plaintiff, but I saw now that it didn't matter. Judge Gabriel wouldn't be taking any evidence.

"I understand your honor," I said.

"Argument?"

Taking my cue from the judge, I made quick work of it, moving promptly to the summation.

"In any case, turning to the construction of a statute, we have to look at the intent of the legislature in adopting the statute. Here, the intent is obvious: to spare the survivor from uncertainty and lack of closure when a body disappears in circumstances that make death the only rational conclusion."

I droned on for four or five minutes on how it is in the public interest to prevent a surviving spouse from being kept from the family assets she would need to pay the bills and move on with her life. But I cut it short when I realized that Judge Gabriel was barely listening.

"You understand that I was recently a part of that legislature?"

"I do, Your Honor."

She didn't want to be lectured on something she understood better than I did.

Heather noticed the same thing, but she reacted differently, insisting vehemently that the law meant exactly what it says and that it was not up to lawyers or the court to interpret well understood terms.

" 'High seas' does not and cannot be interpreted to refer to a local river not half a mile wide where Tarry Justice disappeared."

She talked until she ran out of steam, but that didn't take long. She lacked her usual passion and didn't seem in command of the details.

Anne Gabriel had a litany of probing questions for Heather, the likes of which she hadn't asked me. What made a body of water the "high seas"? Was it its depth? The distance from shore? Did the ruggedness of its weather factor into it? Was the Chesapeake Bay the high seas? What about the Chesapeake Bay in a hurricane? What about the Bay of Fundy, which I knew had the most extreme tidal bore in the world, but which Heather didn't know from Long Island Sound? Heather hadn't made the most elementary inquiry into these and the other questions the judge now threw at her. This was something I had never seen—Heather unprepared for a judge's inquisition. She was quickly exasperated. The judge, her old law school chum, seemed amused.

There wasn't much else to the case, just the single issue that would decide it and we'd exhausted our arguments within an hour. As a signal that the case was over, Gabriel straightened the clutter of papers in front of her.

"I'll take it under advisement," she said, instead of ruling from the bench, and left so abruptly that her dozing bailiff didn't have time to pronounce, "All Rise."

When the door to her chambers shut behind the judge, Heather got up and walked out with only a cursory nod to me. I shook my head. Heather had put up the limp effort of a junior varsity defense. I was going to have to explain to my client something I did not understand.

***

Bobbitt and I slipped into a booth and ordered coffee down the street at Ragtime.

"But we won, didn't we?" Bobbitt said.

She peered at me as if she suspected I would hold back the truth.

"Nobody won; nobody lost. The judge took it under advisement, which means she's going to think about it. That's not unusual."

"What's there to think about?"

It was a good question. This was a one-issue case, which had been teed up for the judge for almost a month.

"I'm sure she hadn't read the briefs."

That was probably true.

"She wants to be careful. She's going to establish a precedent here."

The coffee came and Bobbitt added three teaspoons of sugar to hers.

"Precedent! This hasn't happened in a hundred years, and it probably won't happen again for another hundred!"

Bobbitt's flair for melodrama had come to the fore, but she had a point. It wouldn't be a precedent with much application. It occurred to me that Gabriel was disinclined to make a ruling from the bench because she was teetering between her personal view and what she felt the law required.

"She'll let us know in a few days, maybe a week."

"Do you think that's a good sign?"

"I don't know."

I couldn't read those tea leaves because I had no idea what Anne Gabriel believed in, other than Anne Gabriel.

***

Three days later, Heather and I received the same email from the court, which contained a copy of a terse, formal order.

"Having considered the pleadings, the stipulated evidence and the argument of counsel, the Court is of the opinion that Tarrant Justice's unexplained disappearance into the Potomac River from a moving vessel, his body not having been recovered for more than six months, constitutes sufficient grounds to support a declaration of death and it is so Adjudged, Ordered, and Decreed."

I called Bobbitt to report the news and she was ecstatic, promising to get a check in the mail right away.

"The Order becomes final in twenty-one days. Don't rock the boat."

"Why would I do that?"

Because you are a boat rocker, is what I wanted to say, but I held my tongue and congratulated her again.

Then, I walked over to Ireland's Four Courts to see Phyliss. She seemed glad to see me as she slid a bourbon on the rocks across the bar to me. I had a victory under my belt, nothing to occupy my time, and Phyllis seemed happy to pass the sleepy afternoon chatting with me.

Chapter Fifteen

Who Needs Friends Like These?

The Arlington bar was a petri dish of lawyers: those with strong ideals, others looking for an edge, and a select group with a finely-honed instinct for self-preservation. The trick was knowing the difference, and no one had mastered that art like Heather Burke.

A week or so after my victory in the Justice case, she called and asked if I had time for a cup of coffee. It sounded like old times until she mentioned the location. Willard's was an off-the-beaten track coffee bar that occupied the first floor of a two-story building of the same vintage and quality as DP's cinderblock palace. She periodically used the place when she wanted to turn the screws on witnesses, informants or interested parties, and I had been among them.

My antennae went up, but I agreed. With Heather, it was always better to know what she wanted.

It was a steamy August afternoon. I got there first and had a glass of sweetened iced tea waiting for her when she walked in. She sat down and immediately pushed it away. I noticed dark circles beneath her eyes that she'd tried to conceal with excess make-up.

"How are you?" she said.

I looked at her carefully. She seemed tense and irritable, making me doubly suspicious of her motives.

"I'm alright."

She took a lungful of air.

"Is Rachel Justice still your client?"

"That depends."

"Depends on what?"

"On what you think she did."

She laughed, and I detected a note of insincerity.

"Good answer."

"The real answer is no. The case is over, and she paid me. Unless she needs me to do something after the court's order becomes final."

"But that would just be administrative follow up, wouldn't it?"

"I guess. Unless you've got something else in mind."

I wasn't sure where she was going.

"Well, that's good," she said.

I wondered what she was holding back.

"Is the Commonwealth going to appeal?"

"No, we'll let the ruling stand."

I looked around. The Starbucks down the street attracted most of the afternoon chit-chatters and coffee sippers. Raighne Youngblood, an army vet and PTSD sufferer who, according to rumor, had left his penis in Afghanistan, was behind the coffee bar. Anxious and high-strung, Raighne liked to keep things peaceful, and Willard's patrons, mostly regulars, tended to honor his intolerance of disturbance. The place was as quiet as a church and that was why Heather liked it.

"But you didn't call me here to tell me that."

"No, I didn't."

She put her hands on the table in front of her, her delicate fingers spread apart.

"I came here to hire you."

I straightened up. The tension, the insincere laugh—it all began to make sense.

"Hire me to do what?"

As she leaned forward her voice dropped, though there was no one to overhear.

"It's not easy to talk about. I'm here as an intermediary for someone who's being blackmailed."

"Blackmailed? Isn't that the sort of thing your office usually prosecutes?"

She shook her head at me like a teacher dealing with a slow learner.

"You defended a blackmail case several years ago."

"Yeah. A case called *Kellogg*. I lost that case."

"Yeah. I tried it against you. But everybody lost that case, didn't they?"

I knew what she meant. The express threat in any blackmail effort is that the secret will get out if the authorities are involved. My guy went to jail, but the poor sucker he was blackmailing lost his job and his wife when the ugly facts came out.

"I guess they did."

She nodded somberly.

"Who's the target?"

"I can't tell you that."

My ears pricked up.

"Isn't that the normal starting point?"

"It's someone of some political prominence around here whose name you know."

"I see. And what does the blackmailer have?"

"Sexually explicit video."

I pushed away from the table to gain some perspective.

"With someone who is not the target's spouse?"

"You get it."

I thought for a minute.

"This isn't about you, is it?"

Her face clouded up like a violent thunderstorm primed to unleash its fury. She reached across and slapped me so hard that Raighne leaned over the bar to see if assistance was warranted. I waved him away.

"I deserved that."

I said it, but I didn't mean it. It was a logical assumption and a question that had to be asked. I was glad to know I was wrong.

"Anyway, you think I can help?"

"Among other things, you're a savvy, experienced guy; you're a shrewd negotiator, and you're not connected to my office."

I used her iced tea glass to take the sharp sting out of my cheek.

"I need to know the target."

"No, you need to know the blackmailer."

"I'm waiting."

Heather didn't waste any time.

"Rachel 'Bobbitt' Justice. Your former client."

"Jesus."

I rubbed my temples, anticipating the headache sure to come.

"Yeah, Jesus is right."

"You're kind of putting me on the spot here, aren't you?"

"Sure, but who else can do it? You've got a relationship with her; presumably she trusts you, and she certainly knows you're a good lawyer."

"You want me to take sides against my former client?"

"No, I want you to help her. Look, you know as well as I do that this won't turn out well for her if she persists."

"How much is the demand?"

"There is no demand. That's part of the problem. Bobbitt's smart. She let the target know she has the video. There's no actual threat of what she might do with it."

"I feel better. At least no one's accusing Bobbitt of a crime."

"Not yet. As of now, it's an open-ended threat."

"What does Bobbitt get out of it?"

"She's in a position to manipulate the system. She's got a 'Do Not Go to Jail' card."

"I see. You want me to approach her and see what it will take to get it back?"

She swung away from the table and stared out the window. Heather was struggling with an awkward, piecemeal presentation of the facts, made necessary by her decision to protect the unnamed third party.

"I don't know if money's going to do it. It might be a good place to start, but I'll leave that to your judgment."

"Then you want me to ask her what it will take?"

She leaned forward.

"I want you to get the goddamn video back. Whatever it takes."

"How am I going to do that?"

"That's up to you. The Commonwealth Attorney's office will have your back."

I stared at her for several seconds, most likely with my mouth hanging open like a cod in a net. No lawyer wants to be in the position of needing the protection of the CA's office. The whole thing seemed half baked, dangerous, and rife with obvious risk. And for all these reasons, it intrigued me.

"Money? How am I going to be paid for this?"

"You'll have a powerful friend when this is over."

"You mean the one whose name you won't give me?"

"What's your hourly rate?"

"For this? Three fifty an hour."

She tugged at her chin.

"I happen to know that your rate starts with the number two."

"Not on this case. For this, I charge my fixer rate."

"Just get the video back."

She was asking a lot. This wasn't the sort of caper I could cook up on my own. Besides, I wanted to test her resolve.

"I'll need some help. Someone who knows how to work on the edges."

Her eyes narrowed.

"I'll need DP."

"Works on the edges? He doesn't even know where the lines are."

Twin Killing Private Investigations was technically out of business, but even without a license, DP took on discrete projects that might technically require a license. I often abetted this venal sin, as I had on the Justice matter, and I was always satisfied with his diligence, his instincts, and his persistence. Because my willingness to use DP was an open secret between Heather and me, she had an idea of his skills and discretion.

I raised a hand.

"He made a mistake once and paid a big price for it. But he's a pro. You need someone like him to get this done right."

She exhaled in a huff.

"Okay."

At that moment, I believed she'd agree to any condition I imposed, as long as I got the video back.

"Let me think about it."

"I need to know tomorrow."

"Is there a clock ticking down on this?"

"Of course. It's an extortion case."

I looked at my watch.

"Same time, same place tomorrow?"

She nodded.

"I'll be here."

Chapter Sixteen

Seedier By The Minute

Inside DP's office building, next to the first-floor reception area, was a conference room and two square, non-descript offices—mine, and an identical one leased by Mitch Tressler, a real estate and trust and estates lawyer with even less business than me.

I'd known DP long enough and in a variety of circumstances to appreciate the breath of his gifts. As I arrived back at the office, I heard the dull roar of a vacuum cleaner. I found him in the conference room, tidying up after Mitch. He looked up and turned off the machine.

"About time you cleaned this dump," I said.

"What do you care? You never need it."

"Maybe this is why Mitch never pays his rent on time."

He shrugged, giving me this round. The fencing over, he put his hands on his hips and waited. I gestured toward the stairs.

"I got something for you. You got a few minutes?"

I followed him upstairs, where he took a seat behind his always-cluttered desk, and as he cleared off the faux leather surface, I pulled up a chair.

"By the way, did you fix that tap?"

"Sure did. I disabled the bug in your office. On the phone, they're getting a continuous loop of 1970s disco hits. Won't take them long to get the message."

I laughed and he changed topics, looking hungry for something to do.

"So, what have you got?"

"An unexpected client. Heather Burke."

He whistled shrilly.

"What's she done?"

"Nothing, as far as I can tell. She tried to hire me on behalf on an unnamed individual."

"Tried?"

"I told her I needed your help. And I do. Or more accurately, *she* needs your special skills."

He swiveled his chair away from me so I couldn't read his expression, but I knew he was thrilled. After a moment, he continued.

"Who's the unnamed individual?"

"I don't know."

"She wouldn't tell you?"

"I didn't push it."

"Why not? That's the key, isn't it?"

"No. The key is the underlying problem."

"Blackmail?"

"You got it."

"It's usually something like that when they won't tell you the name. You sure your old girlfriend's not the target?"

"Don't call her my old girlfriend."

"Well?"

I considered DP's question and Heather's answer.

"She says she's not."

"That's what I'd expect her to say."

He shook his head.

"Who's the blackmailer?"

"My former client, Bobbtt Justice."

He rubbed his hands in delight and a grin lit up his face. No complication was too seedy for DP.

"What's Heather doing in the middle of this?"

"You can ask her when you see her tomorrow afternoon."

"Why am I going to be seeing her?"

"I want her to approve what you'll be doing."

"And what's that?"

"Detective work."

He shook his head.

"I want my license back."

"I'm not sure she's got that kind of juice downstate."

"She's got it, if she wants to use it."

"You can ask her about that, too."

***

The following afternoon, we walked toward Willard's together, each alone with his thoughts. There was a covered patio out front, and its tables were empty.

"I wonder how they stay in business," I said.

"You aren't paying attention, are you?"

I looked at DP, irritated.

"It's my job to pay attention," I said.

He shrugged.

"Not always."

Just then, we saw Heather seated in the shadows just inside the front door. As we entered the always dimly lit interior, she and DP exchanged nods like the wary antagonists they were.

"Something to drink?"

She had an agreeable, even friendly tone.

She had an iced tea in front of her. I looked at DP and he shook his head. Then, he rolled up his sleeves to signal that he was ready to get to work. Heather took the cue.

"Did Joth explain the problem?"

DP took a careful look at her as he sat down. He assumed a relaxed posture, as if he'd called the meeting.

"As much as he knows, which isn't a lot."

"He says he needs you."

"He probably does."

"I'm willing to go along with it. And you'll be paid for the work you do."

"Paid by who?"

"Me. I'm the middleman."

DP looked at me, then back at Heather.

"You're asking me to do private detective work and you aren't even telling me who I'll be working for. I'll need my license back."

"We can look the other way."

He shook his head sadly.

"Not good enough."

"I'll do what I can."

He folded his arms across his sinewy chest.

"No. I want it restored."

She recoiled slightly. Heather wasn't used to people imposing conditions on her.

"I can't make any promises. It's not my decision."

"But you can make it happen."

"I'll do what I can," she said. "Once it's over."

DP's dark eyes narrowed.

"I want it back before we get started."

Heather did not react well to threats.

"That's impossible."

I knew of people figuratively walking away from the table in a negotiation, but I'd never seen it actually happen. But that's just what DP did. He shrugged, got up and sauntered out of Willard's without a backward glance.

This was a new experience for Heather, too. As a prosecutor, she usually held the hammer in any negotiation in the form of jail time and she was used to people bending to her formidable will. Not this time.

"I'll be damned," she said.

I thought I heard a hint of admiration in her tone. I took a sip of Heather's iced tea to conceal a grin.

"You're going to have to get him back his license, you know."

"Like hell."

"If you want me, he's part of the package. This is a challenging and difficult case and I'm not going into it without the tools I need."

She put her chin in her hand and drummed her fingers along her pretty jawline.

"That's what it sounds like."

It didn't take her long to think it through.

"Get him back here. Tell him okay."

DP hadn't gone far. I jogged half a block to catch up with him and grabbed his elbow as he was waiting for the light to change at Veitch Street.

"Okay, you win. She'll get you your license back. Let's go back."

I was about to guide him back toward Willard's when he pulled his arm away. DP was merciless when he had an advantage. He shook his head vigorously.

"Not today. When she's got the paperwork in hand."

I stared at him for an anxious moment.

"Let's not push it, DP. She has a lot of power."

"What's she gonna do? Revoke my license?"

The light changed and he stepped out into the crosswalk.

I went back into the restaurant and told Heather what he'd said. She didn't seem surprised. There was nothing more to do or talk about. I left her looking like she needed a stiff drink instead of the unfinished iced tea still in front of her.

***

Heather called two days later to say she had the paperwork. The fast turnaround was a measure of her ability to get things done. I walked up to DP's office and told him the good news. He was behind a crowded workbench at the far end of his office, analyzing the mechanism of a door lock. Among his many skills, DP was also a licensed locksmith.

He looked up skeptically.

"Have you seen it?"

"No, I haven't seen it. I trust her."

He bobbed the almost hairless ridges above his eyes that passed for eyebrows.

"She not a friend anymore, Joth. Not in this case. You need to keep that in mind."

This was a key difference between DP and me. Trusting nothing, he even looked at clients as potential adversaries. Ten minutes later, we were on the way to a hastily scheduled meeting at Willard's.

Out on the street, something DP had said two days earlier popped into my head.

"Last time we were walking over to meet with her, I mentioned that Willard's is never crowded. You said I wasn't paying attention. What did you mean?"

He smirked.

"Land records show that a company called Berry and Barry Realty owns the place. But that's a front. The attorney general's office owns Berry and Barry Realty."

"You mean this place is a . . ."

"A safe house. There are three small apartments upstairs and the coffee bar breaks even, so no one complains."

"I had no idea."

"Stick with me Joth. I know all the secrets. That's my job."

Heather was late, and when she arrived, she looked overheated and annoyed, a potentially volatile combination. She reached into her briefcase and pulled out a thin sheaf of documents secured by a binder clip. The top page was a preprinted form, formally signed and embossed with the state seal: a provisional private investigator's license. DP looked it over with care, then flipped through the stack, one page at a time. The application paperwork began on the second page. Most of it had already been filled in with information transferred from his prior license.

"It's all there," she said, leaning forward. "They already have your prints. All you have to do is drive down to Richmond, get your picture taken, and pay the registration fee. They'll issue the permanent license."

DP knew better than to gloat. He nodded and placed the paperwork face down beside him.

"Now let's get to work," he said, rubbing his hands eagerly. "You want us to get back some video, is that right?"

"Yes."

"Buy it or get it back by other means, if necessary?"

"Yes," she said.

By other means?

I took a moment to form the next question.

"Has the target tried to buy it?"

She hedged, then told DP something different than what she had told me.

"There was some talk."

"They couldn't agree on a price?"

"No, that's not it. It's a practical question. You can stick this stuff on a flash drive. How can you be sure you're getting back every copy?"

"So, this person can't buy it with any certainty of being fully protected?"

"Correct."

DP considered the point.

"And this is a public figure."

Heather nodded and this brought me back to the problem that had bothered me from the start.

"And who's the public figure?" I asked.

"You don't need to know," she said. "Just drop it, Joth."

"Of course, we do," I said. "We don't even know what we're asking for."

"Bobbitt will know what you're talking about."

"We still need to know."

As Heather scowled, DP spoke up.

"She doesn't have to tell us. We already know. The target is Judge Anne Gabriel."

Heather's mouth dropped open in astonishment.

"Is it that obvious?"

"It is now."

"How did you know?"

DP turned over the licensing papers and pointed to the signature appearing at the bottom of the top page. Judge Gabriel had signed, authorizing DP's provisional license.

"And she's the one with the clout in Richmond. She used to be in the legislature."

Heather seemed relieved. She knew we needed to know and now she could deny telling us.

"That's alright," DP said. "At least we know what we're trying to recover."

I took a moment to let this new information settle in.

"How much are we authorized to pay?"

"The hope is you can convince her that her best interest is served by giving it up. That's why I got you involved."

"But that's not true," DP said. "As long as she has a copy, she's got protection if the judge tries to retaliate. If she gives all the copies up, she's naked, so to speak."

"Protection from what?" Heather said.

"Who knows? Gabriel is a powerful woman. A fuckin' ballbuster, if you can believe the street."

Heather's eyes drifted toward the door. She knew Gabriel better than either of us, and she knew that DP was right. She nodded.

"Alright. You need to make sure you get all the copies back. You know what you're looking for and you know who has it. Now, I need you to go get it."

DP turned to me.

"You've got her address, right?"

I nodded.

"She lives in the carriage house behind the Major Pelham Inn out in Aldie."

Heather nodded.

"She got the place in Arlington where her husband used to live on the market."

As DP rubbed his bald head, we gave him time to think.

"We'll get her out of there on some pretext this week," he said. "Then we'll pay the place a visit."

He looked at Heather and bobbed his thin eyebrows conspiratorially.

"We'll need a couple of hours for a thorough search. Ms. Burke, we'll need you to make sure we're not interrupted."

Heather stood up, horrified.

"I didn't hear any of that," she said. "I'm sure that if Joth asks her, she'll give it back. Now, just get the video."

She pushed away from the table and left like she couldn't get out of there fast enough. DP waited until he was sure she was gone, then burst into laughter.

***

The heat of the day had dissipated as DP and I walked out of Willard's, but the DC humidity hung in the air like a fog. Businesses were closing for the day, and the restaurants and bars were attracting the departing crowds of young professionals like moths to a flame, a flame I once found irresistible.

We agreed on Ireland's Four Courts for dinner because it was close and had a quiet nook in the back where we could work through our problem.

A perceptive hostess escorted us to a four-top table in the tiny, paneled Robert Burns Room. Burns, of course, was Scottish, not Irish, and everything in the room was equally faux. The walls were paneled in imitation mahogany, and we sat in front of a fireplace that glowed electrically even in the summer heat. From here, the high octane boasting and glib pick-up lines filtered back to us from the bar as white noise.

A waitress in a black smock flashed a perfect smile at us and asked for drink orders. I had just ordered a Vodka Collins but when I caught DP's look of stern disapproval, I cancelled it and made it club soda on the rocks. It was orange soda for DP. The waitress's smile disappeared. She had us pegged as poor tippers. When she departed, DP stretched his limbs and yawned like a sleepy cat.

"I knew Gabriel was a bitch, but who would have expected this?"

"I did," DP said. "She grew up in this county and had quite a reputation in high school."

"What kind of reputation?"

"Let me put it this way: she was known as Easy A and it wasn't because school came easy to her, which it did, by the way."

"No wonder you weren't surprised."

We mused over this for a moment.

"The break-in idea; I loved that."

"I was just testing her," DP said.

He laughed, showing his irregular teeth.

"But it's a good place to start."

I was also testing him. There was no malice in DP, but he was an adrenaline addict. He enjoyed pushing the envelope, out of an anti-establishment fervor and as a business edge. He liked to see what he could get away with. It had cost him his license once and I was glad to see he wasn't planning to tempt fate on my watch.

"But you stated the problem. If it was a single physical object, the size of a football or bigger . . . well, it's not."

"Right, it could be on a flash drive. Or multiple flash drives. She could keep one in a safe deposit box as security."

I pictured Bobbitt's furrowed brow and her habitual expression of distrust.

"I don't know. She thinks she's smarter than everyone else. Where that leads, I'm not sure, but no, an effort to steal it would be a mistake. If we failed and she found out, it would only make her more likely to use it."

The drinks came and I sipped mine.

"Maybe she already has," said DP.

"Already?"

"Gabriel's the chief judge. She assigned herself Bobbitt's case."

I thought about Gabriel's logic-stretching ruling that the Potomac River constituted the high seas.

"And Bobbitt won. Is that a coincidence?"

I nodded vigorously as the scope of the problem came into focus.

"Maybe that's what's going on. If she's used it once, what's to stop her from using it again? If that's true, Judge Gabriel must be desperate."

"But none of that matters if we get it back."

"It, and all copies."

We lapsed into silence. DP and I ordered shanty Irish food for a pair of working-class men engaged in developing a sordid plot. I knew the prospect should have revolted me, but it didn't. It was dirty work, like scrapping for groundballs on the lacrosse field. I felt fired up by the challenge.

The food came, and we ate in silence as we each pursued our own line of thinking. DP ate with the precision that characterized his professional activities. As I knew from the time of his license revocation, he was a man willing to take chances, but not without calculating the risks with the same exacting care he employed to cut his corned beef and cabbage into perfect squares. The problem was his calculations were sometimes wrong.

"You're going to have to talk to her," he said. "I don't see any way around it."

"You think I can shame it out of her?"

"Or charm it out of her. I've seen you do that before."

"I was much more charming and much younger then," I said, although the idea kindled a warming thought. "You think that's why Heather asked me to get involved?"

"No," he said.

That burst my bubble.

"We're all she's got."

I thought about Bobbitt's typically imperious expression.

"Force her? Shame her? Charm her? I don't see any way through it."

"Talk to her. You'll find a way."

An idea flashed through my mind.

"Jimmie Flambeau owes me a favor."

I explained to DP that when I provided Jimmie with the tip about Nick Grimes' Delaware girlfriend, he had expressed appreciation, even gratitude.

DP's sallow face turned a shade paler.

"You don't want to get tied up with Jimmie Flambeau."

"I'm already tied up with him."

"He can help you alright. Jimmie deals in give and take. That's how he runs his business. But are you sure that's a good idea?"

"Why not? We can be sure he'll put a serious scare into her. That's what Jimmie's good at."

"Yeah, but what's it going to cost?"

"We won't know until we ask."

He let his head wag.

"I don't know. Who knows what he might want in return?"

A grim expression settled over his features.

"Talk to her, Joth. Maybe you could appeal to her patriotism . . . or something."

Chapter Seventeen

Lost At Sea

The law made it easy on me. Judge Gabriel's order became final twenty-one days after it was issued. On the twenty-second day, Bobbitt called, and as Marie announced her, I felt an oily disgust that worsened when I heard the superior tone in her voice.

She didn't beat around the bush. She was all business.

"First of all, you're now a widow. That doesn't usually happen in this manner, and I know you're prepared for this day, but I'm sorry."

"You're right," she said. "I've prepared for this for months. What are the next steps?"

"The next thing is you'll need a probate lawyer."

"I don't need a probate lawyer. Tarry was a sound man of business. He had a will, and everything was in a pour-over trust."

"Who's the trustee?"

I found myself mouthing the name before she spoke it.

"Nicky Grimes."

"Somebody needs to reach out to Grimes and get that process started. Make sure he does it right."

"Can you do that?"

Normally, I would have told her to go to hell, but I had Heather's problem to solve.

"I might be able to look into it."

She brushed past the qualified answer as if a yes was presumed.

"I also need someone to negotiate the sale of Tarry's bank shares to Nicky. Liz says you can do that."

I was more qualified to do that than to oversee the administration of her husband's estate.

"You better come in so we can talk about it. What's a good day for you?"

"The sooner the better."

We set an appointment for Friday morning, when I'd have a chance to pit my persuasive powers against her lack of conscience.

***

Bobbitt wasn't the only one watching the calendar. Late that afternoon, DP walked down from his lair and stopped in.

"The twenty-one days ran yesterday," he said.

He nodded at the calendar on the wall behind my desk. I glanced at it over my shoulder.

"The widow Justice is coming in Friday."

"That woman doesn't let any grass grow under her feet, does she?"

I shrugged. I understood her urgency.

"She always wanted to get it behind her. Maybe she's finally going to."

"Sure. What time is she coming in?"

"Ten. She wanted to wait until after the morning rush."

He shut the door, then sat down and crossed one leg over his knee.

"Have you figured out what you're going to say to her?"

"I've given up on the charm angle."

"You underestimate yourself."

"I appreciate that, but the truth is, I find her revolting."

DP nodded.

"You can't charm someone you don't respect."

"I'll try to buy it first. When she learns that her secret's out, it might put a little fear into her."

"Or a little desperation. If she did use it to leverage the result of her trial, she'd be smart to get out while she's ahead. Gabriel can really hurt her if she's backed into a corner. You could threaten her with that reality."

"The only threat I know is Jimmie Flambeau and you've already counseled against going there."

He winked at me.

"I wouldn't bet against your charm."

"Thanks, but I don't think Bobbitt Justice is susceptible."

***

Practicing law in DC Superior Court was like practicing law in a train station. In a cavernous atrium, people of all walks of life come and go, congregate in small groups, and loiter, cajole, argue, console and separate, while on the big electronic board above the escalator, court room dockets are listed with the efficiency and everchanging uncertainty of train track assignments.

My motion to suppress the results of the search of Lincoln Charlestratons's Audi was heard in Court Room E-3 on Thursday morning. It is a small, efficient, and starkly lit chamber, and by eleven o'clock, Judge Alice McCammon's patience for the trivial and tawdry cases that ran through her courtroom was already running thin.

Sensing the need to get to the heart of the argument, I provided a brief opening statement, outlining my argument, and called Bomba to the stand. Except for an odd reluctance to acknowledge his real name, which was Reginald McLeod, Bomba was the perfect witness.

He was a heavy-set Jamaican immigrant with a deep baritone voice and the lilting accent of the islands. He was sharply but conservatively dressed and brisk, sure of the facts, and good natured in his presentation. After the preliminaries, I called his attention to New Year's Day of that year and asked if he knew Lincoln Charlestraton.

"Oh yeah, he come in a lot."

"Do you see him in the courtroom today?"

He pointed to him beside me at the counsel table.

"Did you have any conversation with him that day?"

"It's New Year's Day. I'm behind the bar and when he come in, I serve him his first Painkiller of the new year. He didn't even have to ask for it. I know what he want coming."

"Did he have another?"

"Yes, he did. And one after that."

"Did there come a time when he appeared to be getting intoxicated?"

"Oh yeah. Linc, he a pleasant drunk. Good humored, you know? But we have a deal. When I see it on his face, I hold my hand out."

"Why do you hold out your hand?"

"For his car keys. He know the routine. And he don't object."

"Did he give you his car keys that day?"

"Yes, he did."

"What did you do with them?"

"I put 'em in my pocket. They were still there when Linc got hisself arrested."

"What happened to them?"

"The police told me to give 'em up. I didn't want to, but he said I could be a conspirator if I didn't."

He raised a big, meaty finger.

"That officer over there."

"What happened then?"

"I gave him the keys and they went straight through Mr. Charlestraton's car."

On cross examination, Bomba indignantly protested the implication that he was aware that cocaine was being sold, or even used, in what he called his shack.

The prosecutor wasted a lot of time with this line of questioning, which was fine with me because she couldn't shake Bomba's insistence that Linc's only set of car keys remained with Bomba.

On my cross-examination, the arresting officer admitted that the car remained locked until he opened it. I objected when the officer attempted to testify to what he found in the glove box of Linc's Audi.

"It doesn't matter what he found," I said, "because they found it through an illegal search and seizure."

It didn't take long for McCammon to agree.

"I'm going to suppress the evidence derived from this search."

She looked at the prosecutor.

"Do you have anything else?"

The prosecutor shook her head bitterly. I'd have liked to have been a fly on the wall when she debriefed the cop.

Linc was appropriately grateful. After promising to promptly pay off his bill, he fairly skipped away from the courthouse, a free man with a clean record. Watching him go, Bomba laughed with vigorous good humor.

"You know, I like that man."

"Why is that?"

"Because he's a happy man; a nice man. Maybe he indulge too much, but he good to be around, you know? Make your day a little brighter."

I felt much the same about Bomba.

"You heading back to the shack?"

He looked at his watch.

"Oh Lord, yes."

"What's for lunch?"

"We got fresh grilled grouper sandwich today."

"You got one for me?"

"Oh my, yes. You meet me there in half an hour."

"Just keep your hands off my keys."

He laughed his big, booming laugh and we both walked off toward our cars.

***

In Salem in 1692, an ancestor of mine had been hung for a crime he did not commit, so I knew that justice is a relative term, a matter of perception and circumstance. I also knew that winning and losing can be subject to similar unfairness—the unpredictable bounce of a lacrosse ball, a shot off or just inside the goal pipe, a referee's split-second judgment on an offside call.

I had grown resigned, if not comfortable, relying on these truths in our society. Lincoln Charlestraton had been caught dealing cocaine and gotten off because a cop was lazy. That was just the way it was. When I assumed the responsibility of correcting injustice, I usually found myself in hot water. I had the right to enjoy a little victory. So, I stopped by the Georgetown waterfront to celebrate Linc Charlestraton's good fortune with a clean conscience.

Although it was summer, it was a Thursday and late for lunch and the bar crowd was sparse. The sound of Bob Marley played through the speakers above a faux tiki bar, where I had just found a stool when Bomba spotted me. He made his way over with his shambling gait, a bright, beguiling smile on his face and carrying a Painkiller in a red plastic cup. He looked as relaxed as Saturday morning in a white terrycloth pullover.

"How you like my shack?"

Some shack. He had done it up in a distressed islands motif, but it occupied part of the first floor of a new mixed-use office building on the Georgetown waterfront. The rent must have been steep, and I wondered where it came from.

"Business is good," I said.

He shrugged.

"Business is business. You did good business today."

"I got the right judge."

"Or Charlie got the right lawyer."

"Charlie?"

"Linc. Sometime, we call him 'Charlie.' "

"Charlestration. I get it. I didn't know you knew him that well."

He shrugged again.

"He come in from time to time."

He gave the impression of a man who accepted as true whatever came his way.

"You got any of that grouper left?'

"Coming right up."

A Painkiller is a tasty and seductive concoction of dark rum, pineapple juice, orange juice and coconut cream and it goes down easy on a summer afternoon. I was on my second when Bomba returned with my lunch. After sliding it in front of me, he leaned his bulk on the other side of the bar and folded his hands on it.

"In my business, it's good to know a man like you."

I remembered hearing Irish Dan Crowley say something like that to me once. Within a few weeks, he had become my best source of business.

"You looked like a man who's been inside a courtroom before."

"Nobody in my business want to be inside a courtroom."

That was true. There were a lot of things that could happen to a citizen inside a courtroom and most of them were bad.

"You got a business card?"

I took a handful out of my jacket pocket and put one on the bar. He picked it up and studied it, turning it over as if the back held a clue to my real identify.

Through a set of French doors, the bar opened onto a patio with a boardwalk and a dock beyond.

"If I could give you a piece of free advice, Bomba, you need to be careful about letting drunks get on boats.

You got lucky on New Year's Day. If somebody gets hurt, it could come back on you."

He peered out the doors then shook his head.

"You talkin' about Nick Grimes?"

He shook his head.

"He wasn't hardly drunk at all."

"I was talking about Tarry Justice."

He emitted a booming laugh.

"Now that man was drunk as a zombie."

This was the same phrase that Linc had used.

"Then, why'd you let him get on the boat?" I said, slightly annoyed.

Bomba leaned further forward and lowered his voice.

"He didn't get on no boat."

I put my drink down.

"What? Then how did he leave?"

"Some woman pick him up."

"Some woman?"

"Yeah."

"Did you get a look at her?"

"It was dark, and she was parked over there."

He gestured out toward Water Street, a good fifty yards away.

"But yeah. She got out of the car to help Tarry get in."

"What kind of car?"

He shrugged as if his recollection was vague.

"Red SUV. Decent looking woman, I'll tell you."

"What's that mean?"

He nodded judiciously.

"Middle-aged woman. Solid, you know? A lot of meat on her."

He bobbed his eyebrows as if we were sharing a lascivious joke.

"What color hair did she have?"

"Blonde hair. I like blonde hair."

"You realize Justice never got home?"

He nodded gravely.

"Why didn't you say anything?"

Bomba opened his hands.

"Because nobody ask me."

He read my expression and softened his tone.

"Look, a bar owner don't want the police asking questions. Especially a bar owner with black skin. As far as I know, he left with his girlfriend."

"Did he have a girlfriend?"

"I don't know nothin' about that."

I saw that Bomba was testing me with this disclosure, measuring my discretion as a potential counsel.

"You know that the person in that car probably killed him?'

He straightened up with great dignity, shaking his heavy head, and I knew that I would never be asked to represent Bomba.

"I don't know nothin' about that."

I drained the rest of my drink and settled up. On the way back to my office, I told myself it didn't matter, that Tarry Justice was undoubtedly dead and had been dead on the day I asked the court to declare him so. But it *did* matter. It just mattered now in a different way.

***

I called DP from my car as I crossed Key Bridge into Virginia and asked him to meet me at Little Rocky Run, a playground not far from the office. He got there first, and I found him in the seat of a swing in an otherwise empty set. I took the adjacent swing. DP was moving like a cautious ten-year old.

"I just had lunch with the guy who owns Bomba's Beach Shack. Bomba himself. He was there on January one. Tarry Justice is dead alright, but he didn't drown."

DP stopped swinging.

After confirming that we were alone, I summarized what Bomba had told me.

DP whistled.

"So, they were in it together. Bobbitt and Grimes."

"Sure looks like it. She gets the money, and he gets the bank."

He rubbed his head, thinking.

"It makes sense," he said. "The boat thing is uncertain. He might not go overboard so easy. He might swim or float, somebody might see him and pull him out of the drink."

"And that's what the police would think too. In fact, it's exactly what they're thinking. Falling off a boat is a common enough accident, but it's a bad way to try to pull off a murder."

I heard myself say that and just kept going.

"Then, where's the body?"

"That's the question, isn't it? Justice was a tall guy, but slightly built, and he was three sheets to the wind. She didn't have any problem getting him into the car."

I paused.

"Then what?"

"Then, she slips him something. A sleeping pill? A shot of Nyquil? It wouldn't have taken much. Then what?"

DP picked up the thread.

"She's going to need some help from there. Grimes is running the boat back to the Pentagon Marina and that'll take some time, but it's a short drive for her. She's probably there before he is."

"Right," I said. "She waits for him in the parking lot, then they take him . . . who knows where . . . to finish it."

"No," said DP.

He shook his head.

"Too messy and too risky. He might come to; a cop might pull them over. And where are they going to dump the body?"

"They'd probably already dug a grave somewhere."

"I don't think so. It's January and the ground's frozen and that's a tough enough chore in the summer. No, he's supposed to have drowned in the Potomac, and that's exactly what happens. They weigh him down with something and watch him sink."

"In the marina basin?"

DP started swinging again as he thought about it.

"Probably not. That marina gets dredged occasionally. But just outside it. Maybe they put him back in the boat, take him under one of the bridges and dump him in. And if he turns up someday, nobody will think twice about it, because that's where the guy's supposed to be."

I shook my head to drive away the disturbing image.

"That's ugly."

"It is. And Mrs. Justice is even more dangerous than we thought. You'll have to report this to the DC police."

DP lost me there. The last thing I wanted was someone dragging the river.

"That's not my job. Or yours."

"I thought you cared about justice?"

I also had Judge Gabriel's problem to think about.

"Right now, I care about getting that video back. And we need to deal with Bobbitt Justice to get that."

"Well," he said. "This might make it easier."

"Yes, it might," I said. "But it could also make it harder. Once she realizes we know what happened to Justice, she'll never give it up. More than ever, it will be her ace in the hole."

He rubbed his eyes.

"You know Joth, I haven't always chosen right over wrong, and that's how I lost my license, but at least I've always known the choice I was making. It's scary when you can't tell them apart."

He looked at me shrewdly, seeking a reaction, a tell—not because he wanted an acknowledgment of guilt or a statement of contrition. He'd understood what had happened to Track from the day he disappeared. He was judging the sturdiness of my commitment to the righteousness of what I'd done.

There was no need to deceive DP Tran because he would have done the same thing I did. Or at least that's what I wanted to believe.

"You know what I mean?"

"I know," I said.

DP nodded at me.

We shared a world view that sometimes put us at odds with the mores of the society we lived in. But we both believed it and we both owned it. The only difference was, I was living it.

Chapter Eighteen

Going Rogue

The Bobbitt Justice who stepped into my office on Friday morning presented herself entirely differently from the stylish, county-club wannabe who had brought an arcane legal problem to me in June. She was firm, direct, and lacking any of the girlish mannerism she had expected to beguile me with on her previous visits. Once again, she brushed away the condolences I'd delivered on the phone.

I resettled myself in my chair.

"Mrs. Justice . . ."

"Bobbitt."

"Mrs. Justice."

I looked at her squarely.

"Before we get down to your business, there's something we need to talk about. It's come to my attention that you've got something that you shouldn't have. Something that could be harmful to a friend of mine."

I picked my next words with care.

"And something that might implicate the criminal justice system."

It took her a moment to process this, then she smiled, cold as ice.

"I knew she was an acquaintance of yours. I didn't know she was a friend."

"A colleague, then. It doesn't matter. I need to get it back, Mrs. Justice. Keeping it will only result in trouble for a lot of people and you'll certainly be one of them."

"Is that a threat?"

She asked sweetly, as if she might throw me off my game.

"There's no purpose in making a threat, Mrs. Justice. You know that."

"You are a resourceful and competent man, Mr. Proctor. Are you doing this at her direction?"

"At her request. I don't want it to escalate beyond that."

"Aren't you *my* lawyer?"

"Not yet. Not on this matter. Our case is over. But if we can get this resolved, I'll take care of the estate and the stock transfer issues without further charge to you."

"This is getting interesting," she said.

She was as unperturbed as if we were discussing a bridge hand.

"You can hurt somebody, but that somebody has powerful friends. You don't want to force the issue."

I was making reasonable points in a reasoned tone, and she responded with similar dispassion.

"But if I give it up, doesn't that put me at risk?"

"No."

I spoke with a little more vehemence than I should have allowed.

"Your fingerprints aren't on it, literally or figuratively. I'll destroy it and there will be nothing more said."

"I think I can trust you, but can I trust her?"

"I'll just tell her that the problem is solved. I'll be your lawyer again and bound by confidentiality."

She processed what I said and flashed a smile of victory.

"She must be quite nervous about this."

"This is a day for putting things behind us, Mrs. Justice. I don't need to remind you that you start your new life today. Don't drag a set of messy problems into it. Put it behind you and she'll do the same thing."

"You can guarantee that?"

"Yes, I'll tell her that it's part of the price for the return of the item."

She tossed her head and gave it some thought, which produced a smile.

"I suppose it has served its purpose, hasn't it?"

Throughout this negotiation, each of us were dealing from information unknown to the other. She couldn't know if I was aware of the extent of her felony, or how much I knew about her extortion scheme. At the same time, her cool response made me wonder if she held a trump card.

"I'm not sure that it has," I said.

"Come now, Mr. Proctor. The Potomac River is hardly the high seas. Don't you agree?"

I was horrified, and my face probably gave it away. DP's speculation was accurate. Bobbitt had used the video to extort a favorable ruling from Judge Gabriel. The thought was appalling, but I let that go. There was too much left to do.

"I take it you're now willing to give it to me?"

"I didn't say that. I might be willing to *sell* it."

"And for how much?"

"Let the bidding begin," she said.

Her haughty self-confidence sickened me.

"I need assurances that I have every copy."

"Of course."

I processed her lack of enthusiasm.

"Here's what I can promise. If we reach a deal on money, I'll pledge to you that I'll destroy all copies of the video you give me and say nothing to anyone. If necessary, I'll say that no such video ever existed. But if another video turns up, that'll be different. I'll become the main witness against you."

She nodded placidly.

"And you'll take care of my remaining legal issues?"

"After we take care of this little item."

"I want the payment in cash."

"Of course."

"One payment."

She struck me as someone who'd keep pushing until I said no.

"Let's not get ahead of ourselves. I'll get you a number. It'll be a reasonable number. There shouldn't be any reason for back-and-forth negotiations."

Her face soured. She got the message, but I knew I'd have to go another round or two with her before I closed the deal.

"Is there anything else, Mr. Proctor?"

"Not today."

I stood up and walked her to the outside office door and stood by Marie's desk, watching her until she got into her vintage Mercedes and drove away.

Marie didn't smoke or drink, and had no vices, as far as I knew. I was usually suspicious of people who claimed adherence to puritanical virtue, but she didn't broadcast her positions and didn't judge me, and I valued her opinion of others.

"What was that all about?" she said.

I thought of DP. Among his many lessons was the observation that to most people a receptionist is hardly more alive and no more perceptive than a potted palm, but that you can learn a lot about your business visitors from a receptionist who pays attention.

Marie was a competent typist and only adequate on the phone, but she was watchful as a hawk. She had seen them come and go over the years: lowlifes and criminals of every type and description, those who'd made mistakes, those who'd caved to pressure, and those who lacked the moral compass to care. Her insight and access to my files put her in a rare position to form opinions of those who came in and out of my office.

"I take it you don't like her?"

"There was something different about her today," she said.

I thought about her careless choice of clothes and lack of makeup.

"She's no longer interested in her image."

"I mean, she was talking to herself."

"When?"

"When she first came in."

Marie gestured toward the frayed couch across from her desk.

"Her husband died six months ago. She lives alone. People like that talk to themselves."

"Do you want to know what she said?"

I sat down on the same couch Bobbitt had occupied.

"Yeah."

"Has she got something that could put a friend of yours in *The Washington Post*?"

I pinched my nose and closed my eyes.

"Is that what she said?"

"That's what it sounded like to me."

"I hope the answer to that question is no."

I got up and went back to my office, thankful that I'd already emptied and disposed of the office bottle.

***

An hour later, I heard a knock at my door. It was DP, who never knocked. I'd never seen such a glowing smile on his face.

"Can I come in?"

"Of course."

He winked and pulled the door shut behind him. As he approached my desk, he removed a small hiking bag from his shoulder, unzipped it, and took out a Ziplock bag. He spilled its contents across the leather surface of my desk: seven identical flash drives, each affixed with a typewritten label. I picked one up to read.

"Fleming" it said, along with a date.

"What does this mean?"

"It means Bobbitt Justice is out of business."

"Out of business! Where did you get this?"

He shifted his weight to make sure the door was closed.

"Challenging times call for extreme measures. I knew she'd be here with you, so I paid a little visit to Bobbitt's house today."

"You broke in?"

I could feel my eyes bulging.

"It wasn't hard," he said, grinning. "She lives in the converted carriage house at the back of the Major Pelham Inn. It's quite charming. I waited in the woods for her to leave this morning and took care of business. The lock was easy."

I shook my head.

"What if she had cameras? You could be putting yourself into her hands."

"What's she gonna do? Go to the police?"

He nodded at the pile of flash drives on my desk.

"Not after what I've found."

DP picked them up and let them sift through his fingers like a miser flaunting his gold. I tried to find a measured tone as I worked through my thoughts.

"You did a lot in one morning."

"That's not all. She's got a couple of hidden cameras set up in the honeymoon suite in the inn."

"Honeymoon suite?"

That was the room Heather and I had stayed in many years ago.

"Yeah."

When DP was done pawing the merchandise, I picked them up, one after another, examining the label on each. None of them contained Anne Gabriel's name. DP had put together a handwritten index of the flash drives, which I scanned quickly.

"Robbins, Swan, Toynbee, Peacock, DelTorchio and Blodgett."

Some of the names were too common to identify; one could have been a state delegate; another the managing partner of one of the county's biggest law firms.

"Sounds like a flock of birds, but no Gabriel," I said. "How do you explain that?"

"I was in a hurry. I didn't look at the names until I got out of there."

"So, there could be others?"

"I don't think so. It's a small place and I turned it up-side down. Maybe she used the name of Gabriel's partner."

"Why would she do that?"

He had no answer for this and neither did I.

"Have you viewed any of these?"

"No."

He replied with a squeamishness that didn't surprise me. For all his rough edges, DP was something of a prude. He rubbed his eyes.

"Well, let's keep them in your safe until we figure out what to do with them."

"When are we going to do that?"

I felt a bit like DP had brought me the gift of an armed bomb. I didn't know what to do with those purloined videos, if that's what they were. At least for the moment, they were more dangerous than useful.

"We better sleep on it."

I gathered up the flash drives, carefully wiped my fingerprints from them and dropped them into a plastic bag. DP put it into his hiking bag.

"Let's talk about it over lunch tomorrow," I said. "I hope you'll come up with some good ideas by then."

***

I was getting ready to leave for the day when the phone rang. I assumed it would be an indignant and overwrought Bobbitt. Exhausted, my first reaction was to let it roll over to voicemail, but I knew I'd have to talk to her sooner or later. I took a deep breath and picked up the receiver.

It wasn't Bobbit. It was the last person I expected. It was Melanie Freeman.

Always soft spoken, Melanie's voice was quieter than usual. She sounded unsure of herself and, I thought, lonely. After we'd shared a few pleasantries, I asked her if she was working.

"It's my night off."

"What are you doing?"

"I bought two pieces of fresh swordfish today. That's one too many for me."

I let this sink in.

"Can I bring anything?"

"You can bring a bottle of wine. Or maybe two."

"Okay."

I turned off my cell phone and left my office.

***

There's no secret to cooking fresh swordfish. Baste it in butter and cook it ten minutes per inch in a very hot oven, flipping it once. Serve with lemon. But Melanie managed to overcook it. She didn't even realize it and I didn't care. Neither of us was there for the swordfish.

We'd finished the first bottle of wine over dinner and were on to the second one by the time we worked our way to the daybed. She didn't kiss like an altar guild lady. She kissed like a woman who needed to go to confession.

"We need to slowdown," she said.

I had the first two buttons on her shirt undone and was in no mood to stop.

"Why?"

"We need to think about what we're doing."

"I think we both know what we're doing."

"It's a big step."

"You can be a little less than pure for one night."

"Venial sins lead to greater sins."

"Don't you ever do anything without thinking about that? The Pope doesn't care about what we're doing. You need to get church business out of your head."

She slapped my hands away and sat up. I had crossed the line by disparaging the belief system that held her life together.

"Church business is important. You've had a peek at that."

I assumed she meant the church financial records she'd caught me surreptitiously reviewing on her computer on the day I'd picked her up for lunch.

"So, Nick Grimes is behind on his contributions. Big deal. He's done a lot worse than that."

"Don't joke."

"I'm not joking."

"I thought he was your friend."

Tarry Justice had been a bit player in this drama, dead before I'd been introduced to the rest of the cast. Yet, bit by bit, glimpses of him had emerged: a hard worker, protective of family assets, a teetotaler. He was not part of Father John's church family but might have been the victim of one of them—a victim of his own business partner.

"That was a ploy. I've learned a lot about Nick Grimes and some of it is ugly. I wanted to know more."

"Why do you care?"

"Because somebody's dead and I want to know who's responsible."

Her eyes widened.

"Dead?"

"Yeah. As in mortal sin."

I was trying to be facetious, but the barb didn't stick.

"What happened?"

"It's in the past, Melanie."

In the throes of sexual frustration, I had pushed it too far. I tried to back pedal.

"Let's just forget about it."

"Does it have to do with the church?"

I ignored her and tried to run my hand up her skirt, but she pushed me away.

"No. It's a personal matter. It's got nothing to do with the church."

She stood up and smoothed down her skirt and then rebuttoned her blouse.

"But it does, doesn't it? I should tell Father John. He could help."

"Help who?"

"Help Mr. Grimes. If he did something bad, Father John can help him."

I got up and approached her like a wrestler looking for an opening.

"Forget about Nick Grimes. He's not worth it."

"Are you telling me the truth about this?"

She looked sad and confused and I felt for her. She was a simple, decent woman, trying to do the right thing, and I didn't meet enough of that breed.

I took a breath and sat on the edge of the daybed, wondering how I'd allowed myself to get into this position.

"Look, Maybe Nick Grimes needs some spiritual consolation. Maybe we all do. But that's up to him, don't you think?"

"The people who need it the most don't always ask for it."

Melanie had a way of stumbling onto the truth without realizing it.

As I sat wearily on the edge of the bed, I felt her attitude toward me suddenly change, as if she were seeing us as two people simply responding to their human needs.

Perhaps I had completed my penance.

Chapter Nineteen

Fork in the Road

The next morning, Bobbitt arrived at my office, unannounced. She strode past Marie, who was too startled to stop her. She entered my office and slammed the door.

She had me at a disadvantage, as was her intention. Having nothing on my calendar, I was dressed in Bermudas, a loose-fitting polo that had seen better days, and flip flops. She sat and stared at me, her dignity affronted, waiting for a reaction. What came across my face was amusement, not because I intended this reaction, but because I enjoyed the show of wounded pride from a blackmailer caught in the act.

"Good morning, Mrs. Justice. I don't think you were on my calendar today."

I took my time to sit down.

"Cut the crap Joth; you know why I'm here."

"I'm afraid I have no idea, but I gather it's important."

"You broke into my house yesterday morning."

She was carrying an oversized handbag and I suspected a tape recorder.

"Don't be silly. Yesterday morning I was sitting here with you."

"Or had your thugs do it."

"I don't employ thugs. Do you, Mrs. Justice?"

That didn't faze her. And since her immediate broadside had failed, she quickly altered her tone and tactics.

"Somebody broke into my house yesterday and I'm going to the police."

I gave her my most professorial nod.

"That's what people usually do when someone breaks into their house. If you're here to ask my advice, I think you should do the same thing. Provided you have nothing to hide."

She dropped her eyes and considered her options. She'd had a long drive to think through her moves and I was surprised to find her at a loss.

"Anything taken?"

"We had a negotiation; to make a deal."

"Since when is blackmail a negotiation?"

"Blackmail?"

The offended dignity returned.

"I made no demand, and I didn't threaten anyone. I had something you wanted, and we were discussing a price."

"I suppose you just collect them, like some people collect stamps."

"That's right; I don't use them. What do you collect, Mr. Proctor?"

"Speeding tickets."

I was trying to be brusque and offensive, but she didn't miss a beat.

"Then we're quite a lot alike after all, aren't we? We ignore the law to satisfy our own needs and to suit our own sense of justice."

Bobbitt was fond of cooking up sophomoric statements glossed with a tone of profundity, but her strategy made me wonder if she'd heard rumors about my recent past. I growled, aiming to push past it.

"Are you equating speeding with extortion?"

She leaned toward me.

"Once you start making your own law, the details no longer matter."

"It's only a short jump from the theoretical to the consequential, is that what you're saying, Mrs. Justice? Such as using those videos?"

"Only if I felt the need. We use the tools available to us."

She'd hit on something that resonated, and I wondered if she recognized it. Once you take the law into your own hands, you lose the right to claim moral indignation. And I knew that my own guilt was at least as great as hers, although she couldn't know this.

"But you no longer have the asset," I said.

She rose theatrically to her full height.

"As a matter of fact, I do. At least I have a copy of the one you want. You still want me to go to the police?"

I shook my head and chuckled softly.

"I only want what's best for you, Mrs. Justice."

"I'm sure," she said.

The bitterness in her voice did not go unnoticed.

"And how do I know you've still got it?"

"I'll make a copy for you to review if you like. Of course, your little friend won't like that."

"Or she can review it herself."

Bobbitt ignored the point.

"I'll tell you what I'll do. I'll sell it to you for twenty-five-thousand dollars and I'll give you forty-eight hours to produce the cash. No negotiation, no discount."

"And if my client doesn't agree?"

"I think Joyce Morrow at the *Post* would be interested. This is the sort of story that sells newspapers."

She met my eyes.

"Small bills, not consecutively numbered. When you've got it, you tell me. I'll pick a place for you to meet me."

"And how can I be sure you won't keep a copy?"

"Mr. Proctor, you just broke into my house. I'll overlook that little detail, but it's not *you* who should be wondering if you can trust *me*."

She got up abruptly, and with her chin in the air, made her way imperiously out of my office, past the reception desk and out the front door. I followed her as far as the door to my office, where I leaned on the door jam and watched her depart. Then, I noticed Marie, with the eraser tip of a well-chewed pencil between her teeth, pondering me. I nodded toward the street door.

"What do you think of her now?"

"I don't think she'd kill anybody. Not unless she felt she had to."

I laughed.

"*Had* to?"

"You know, if she thought someone let their dog poop on her lawn or something."

I sighed and looked again toward the door.

"She wants me to trust her."

"How much is at stake?"

"She could ruin someone's life."

"Someone innocent?"

I weighed what she probably meant, but I already knew the answer.

"Nobody's innocent."

Marie shook her head sadly.

"There has to be another way."

I took the stairs two at a time up to DP's office, where I found him listening intently to the police band on his ham radio. He held up a hand. I'd come in in the middle of the report.

"They fished a body out of the Potomac," he said.

I felt my knees buckle and sat down.

"They haven't identified the body yet."

Maybe not, but I knew who it was: Track Racker. I'd been waiting for this day since the moment I put him there.

"What part of the river?"

"Hunting Creek. Just south of the airport."

Or maybe not. The river ran south. Over time, objects in the bed of the river moved in that direction, if they moved at all. Just south of the airport was well to the north of where Track went in.

"Tarry Justice?"

"Might be."

We listened until the report wound down.

"What's next?" I asked.

I knew the routine, but hearing it out loud gave me a chance to consider the possibilities.

"They've taken him to the morgue. They'll run the usual tests."

"How long will that take?"

"It won't take long to figure out who it's not. If it's Justice, he's gonna be pretty decomposed."

"Yeah, eight months on the bottom of the Potomac will do that to you. Can you run this down?"

"Nothing to do until they start doing the work."

"Do you know somebody down there?"

He looked at me as if I'd asked him if he knew the name of the first president. His lack of urgency calmed me, and when he stood up, stretched his back, and walked over to the long worktable in the middle of the room, I followed and stood beside him. He'd been preparing marketing materials marked "For Immediate Distribution."

DP maintained sophisticated printing software on his computer that allowed him to concoct phony business cards, IDs and who knows what else. I sat down and slid across a draft of one of the documents he was working on.

In a format appropriate for LinkedIn, it read in bold letters across the top: "Experienced investigator specializing in insurance fraud, locates, domestic relations and crime." What followed was a summary of his practice, with blurbs touting some of his many successes.

"You think that covers it?" I asked.

"It hits the high points. I'm like you. I take what comes in, provided it's interesting."

I turned back to the flyer and continued reading.

"References from prominent local attorneys available on request."

I looked up inquisitively.

"That's you," he said.

DP flashed an impish smile.

"I didn't know I was prominent."

"You will be after we take care of this case for Easy A. She'll owe you."

"Oh, so I'll be blackmailing her next?"

"She'll be grateful."

"I don't think so. She's going to bury this case so deep in her memory banks that hypnotism won't recall it. That's the problem with the business we're in, DP. It isn't like personal injury work, where you can brag about the big recovery you got for your client. Our biggest success stories are forgotten like they never happened. The clients want it that way."

DP looked chagrined. He was usually more hard-headed and realistic than me, but he'd let the excitement from the unexpected renewal of his license get the better of him.

"Well, we'll still have friends on the bench and in the prosecutor's office. That can't be a bad thing."

"I suppose not."

"Which is why you came up here?"

"Nope. I came up to talk about powerful enemies, not powerful friends. Mrs. Justice just came by."

He was about to speak when something clicked and I interrupted him.

"Wait a minute. Peacock! Where are those flash drives?"

I gestured toward his safe.

"Can you get 'em out?"

He walked to the far corner of the long room, where he squatted down and spun the dial on his safe. When it popped, he opened it, reached in, and removed the Ziplock bag containing Bobbitt's spoils. I emptied it on the worktable and pawed through them, looking at each name tag. I held up the one that said Peacock.

"This may explain why there's no Gabriel here. Peter Peacock is the name of Heather's husband."

My heart sank as the likely truth dawned on me, not because I'd failed to see the truth, but for Heather's sake. No wonder she'd sounded so defeated.

"She told us it was Gabriel."

I thought back to our meeting at Willard's when DP had noticed the endorsement on his provisional license.

"No, she didn't. You're the one who jumped to that conclusion and Heather didn't deny it. I thought it was sharp detective work at the time. But really, you gave her an out and she took it."

"So, Heather got Gabriel to sign it?"

"Standard procedure. The license requires the endorsement of a judge."

He flopped into his chair.

"You think it's a video of Heather's husband?"

"It makes sense."

"With another woman?"

"Or another man. You're going to have to take a look at it. See what she's got."

"Why me?"

"Because you're the detective."

He shook his head, trying to avoid the subject.

"I don't even know what he looks like."

"But you can find out. That's what you do."

The whole sour prospect turned my stomach.

"I need you to do this, DP. I'll be in my office."

***

An hour later, I was still processing the day's events when DP came down. He didn't look at me as he came in.

"It's him?"

"Peter Peacock?"

He nodded glumly.

"Yeah, it's him. And it's bad."

229

"How bad?"

He walked to the window and looked out with his hands on his hips.

"Well, the audio quality is good, and the video is excellent."

Then, with a decisive gesture, he pivoted toward me.

"It's kinky, Joth. And they talk about Heather."

I felt the blood drain from my face.

"What do they say?"

"You know, what she does, what she doesn't do. This woman in the video? There's nothing she won't do."

I held up my hand to stop him, but he'd thought it through and continued.

"And another thing. I think I know the woman. I think you know her, too. She's one of Heathers assistants. Sue something."

"Not Sue Cranwell?"

"Dark hair, young and pretty?"

I nodded.

"Well, it sure looks like her. And he calls her Sue."

I put my head in my hands as DP continued to lay it out.

"This explains why Heather put up such a limp defense to Bobbitt's claim. Gabriel didn't fix the case. Heather did. She could have cross-examined Grimes about how drunk he was and about how much cocaine he'd used. We've both seen Heather cut tough witnesses to pieces. By the time she was through with Grimes, there wouldn't have been anything left of him but bones. Gabriel wouldn't have believed a word he said. But she didn't. She let his evidence go in on an affidavit."

I felt a migraine coming on.

"And then, when Gabriel quizzed her on the meaning of high seas, she was totally unprepared. She had to know those questions were coming, and she hadn't even thought about it. Gabriel had no choice in how she ruled."

"Maybe," I said.

As I digested this stream of grim news, I remembered how hard Heather had battled me on the discovery motion. But she'd seemed to give up when Gabriel overruled her request for the prenup. After that, she'd issued no discovery requests, developed no evidence, and stipulated to almost everything.

"Bobbitt must have put the squeeze on Heather between the discovery motion and trial."

DP frowned.

"That's the point Heather made about blackmail in our first meeting at Willard's."

"What point?"

"Everyone loses."

DP nodded, his thought process tracking mine.

231

"If so, Bobbitt's really got her on the griddle. Not only does she have a video that'll make Heather a laughingstock; she can show that Heather dumped the case."

"She wouldn't dare make that argument," I said. "That would put her in jail."

"You think Heather wants to take that chance? She'd lose her job."

"Lose her job?" I said. "She'd be disbarred."

"But we've got the videos. Her days of pulling the strings are over."

Then, I dropped Bobbitt's latest bomb; the thing I'd gone up to talk to DP about before this wave of events distracted me.

"She says she has another copy of the video we want. She wants twenty-five thousand dollars for it."

"She gave you a number?"

I nodded.

DP shook his head.

"She's bidding against herself. She's lying. She hasn't got it."

On another day, this revelation might have given me cold feet, but I saw it from a different angle now. This was my chance to protect Heather and re-earn her trust and confidence.

"Maybe. Probably. But how can we be sure?"

That was where we were, mired in a game of bluff.

"Okay, DP, who is supposed to be the best poker player in the county?"

He tilted his head in thought, but it didn't take long.

"That would be a mistake."

"But that's what this has become now, right? A game of high stakes poker?"

"Don't do anything stupid, Joth."

***

Before I could reply, Marie buzzed in and announced a call: Heather Burke.

I gestured for DP to shut the door and put the call on speaker.

"Are you alone?"

She sounded subdued and apologetic.

"Of course."

DP nodded and put his finger to his lips.

"I suppose you know the police pulled a body from the river this afternoon?"

"Yeah, I just heard about. Tarry Justice?"

"No. It's a fresh body."

Fresh body?

Tarry Justice had been feeding the rockfish since New Year's Day, hadn't he? And if it wasn't Justice, did this mean that Track Racker had finally surfaced?

I couldn't find my voice as I heard Heather swallow.

"It's tough to know for sure right now," she said, "but the coroner thinks it's Nicholas Grimes."

Nicholas Grimes!

I was stunned. So was DP. He froze like a corpse. I took a deep breath.

"Nick Grimes? The banker? What happened?"

"It looks like suicide. He left a note."

I knew I needed to ask follow-up questions with care.

"What did the note say?"

"It said he killed his partner."

"Tarry Justice? He killed Tarry Justice?"

"Yup. Got him drunk and threw him off his boat on New Year's Day. Hit him on the head with a winch first, whatever that is."

"Anything else?"

She sighed.

"Yeah. He talked about what a fine lady Mrs. Justice is and that he's been swimming in remorse because he deprived her of her life partner for selfish reasons. *Swimming in remorse*. That's the phrase he used."

I focused on a different word.

"The selfish reasons being?"

234

"That he wanted the bank."

"Wow."

I needed space to think.

Grimes had called her an elegant lady during our meeting at Saigon Breeze, but he didn't seem guilt ridden. Or did he feel the heat closing in? Or was it Bobbitt who felt the heat? In any case, if Grimes had killed himself, he had shielded Bobbitt Justice from culpability with his last act on Earth.

"So, you were right," Heather said. "Justice is dead, and his wife got the declaration she deserved. No hard feelings?"

"Of course not."

The words trailed out automatically. There was so much more to it than that.

"I've been pretty rough on you" she said. "And I'm sorry."

She's holding something back.

Heather was not in the habit of apologizing for anything and she certainly didn't go out of her way to do so. But I knew something about her that she didn't know I knew. I nodded at DP and picked up the phone. He took the hint and quietly left the room.

"So, you were right," she said. "I guess."

"What do you mean, you 'guess?' "

"I don't know. It seems a little too pat to me, the suicide story."

"In what way?"

"I'm not sure. It didn't feel like a suicide note. It felt like a high school kid's version of a suicide note."

"How so?"

"A little long on the melodrama; let's just say."

I focused on the use of the verb *swimming* and the noun *remorse*, and the phrase *life partner*. I tended to agree. The only people who spoke that way before killing themselves were Shakespeare's tragic heroes.

"Where'd you find it?"

"That's another thing. His priest brought it over."

"His priest? Father John Tedesco?"

"Yeah, and I know you know him and don't like him, so don't jump to any conclusions."

"What conclusions should I not jump to?"

She ignored the question.

"You know where he found it, or where he says he did? Under the windshield wiper of his car."

"Where was his car parked?"

"In his spot in the lot at St. Carolyn's."

"So, Grimes, on his way to throw himself in the river, stops by the church to put a suicide note on his priest's car window?"

"Yeah, that's how the story adds up."

236

"How 'bout the handwriting?"

"It was printed off a computer."

"But he signed it?"

"Nope, the signature was printed, too."

I made sure that Heather could hear me exhale.

"Why are you calling me?"

I knew the answer already.

"Because you know him. And I'm trying to figure him out."

Him, I realized didn't mean Grimes. It meant Father John.

"Yeah, I know him a little."

"You don't like him. Tell me why."

I'd caught him embezzling petty amounts of money from the church back in the spring, but I wasn't going to tell Heather that, at least not yet.

"I'm probably the only criminal defense lawyer he knows. So, if you're thinking about charging him with something, maybe you want to stop talking to me."

She sighed.

"I was hoping you wouldn't say that."

"Why?"

"I'm not thinking as clearly as usual these days, Joth. I was hoping to get some help from you."

"Help on what?"

"On what to do next."

She was vulnerable and my heart went out to her. I wanted to help but without getting my feet too deep in the water. I didn't know anybody else who spoke in such grandiose language. *Swimming in remorse*? There was only one conclusion I could come up with and it stunned me. Father John Tedesco had forged that suicide note, then claimed he found it on his car. But why?

John hadn't hired me and there was no certainty he would, even assuming Heather stirred up trouble for him. I owed her a lot and didn't owe John Tedesco or Bobbitt Justice a damn thing, but something wouldn't let me put him on the griddle.

No, the way to help Heather was to address the bigger problem that was dragging her down—the risk that Bobbitt Justice posed to her professional existence.

"Let me think about it, Heather. Why don't you just let it sit for a day or two? I'm sure things will look better by then."

"Can I call you? Maybe on Monday?"

"Of course. And Heather? On the other thing? I'm pretty sure I'll have some good news for you by then."

I heard her sigh.

"You think so?"

"I'm sure of it."

"We'll have a cup of coffee. Maybe you can help me think some things through."

"Sure."

"Like we used to do when everything seemed simple."

I was glad DP had left the room. When I hung up, I was fighting back tears. Heather needed me now. I was the only person who could help her and that was all that mattered.

Chapter Twenty

Dealing with the Devil

Jimmie Flambeau was a gambler and bookie by profession, but his knack for swiftly collecting legally unenforceable debts made him in demand with those who operated on the fringes of the law . . . or well outside it. He never promised more than he could deliver, and he delivered where others without his reputation could not.

By contrast, Irish Dan Crowley floated like an oversized sprite around the edges of all that was illicit but not illegal in Arlington County. But above all else, Dan was a sensible, practical man. He kept his hands scrupulously clean. And he was fundamentally honest. That was the basis of our professional relationship.

It was two o'clock. I drove down to Dan's gentleman's club in Crystal City. The lunchtime crowd had thinned out and the congressman were all back on the Hill. Dan was behind the bar, leaning on his elbows while he explained the finer points of something to one of his dancers, who was seated on a stool across from him, killing time between sets. He straightened up when he saw me. The girl turned as well and instinctively pinched her negligée closed at her throat. Then she smiled. Dawn was a former friend of Jenny. Dan shooed her away and I occupied Dawn's warm and sweaty stool.

"Beer?"

He was already drawing one and quickly slid it in front of me.

"You've got something on your mind," he said.

"I've got something going on and I think I'm going to need some special help."

Dan opened his bearlike paws.

"I'll do what I can."

I shook my head.

"The kind of help that only Jimmie Flambeau can provide."

He stared at me solemnly for a long moment.

"You know what you're doing?"

"That's why I came to see you, Dan. There's really no other way."

He pinched his lips together as he sized me up, then picked up my beer and led me to an empty booth. He slid into his spot and waited for me to begin.

"You've warned me to stay away from him in the past, but you and Jimmie are friends."

"Jimmie's like a certain kind of dog. He can be a good friend, but you gotta treat him careful. Me, I run a strip club. I need a dog like that."

"Seems like it's worked out for you."

"Jimmie's never lied to me; I can tell you that."

"He's your friend. How about to other people?"

He tossed his head, seeming to give my question some consideration. I didn't think he was contemplating *what* to say; just how he was going to say it.

"No. Jimmie does what he says he's going to do. That's the difference between him and the police. The police, they tell you one thing and when you do what they tell you to do, they come in and tell you something else. They forget all about what they told you the first time. But what are you gonna do about it? They got the handcuffs. With Jimmie, it's different. Being reliable, not honest, necessarily, but reliable, is how he stays in business. Of course, be usually doesn't have to do the things he promises, but that's because people know he will if they cross him."

"How come everybody's so scared of him? He had to do something to get that reputation."

Dan folded his hands, looked over his shoulder conspiratorially and leaned in toward me.

"He cut his teeth making book for Virginia Tech kids down in Blacksburg," he said, in a dramatic whisper. "You know that."

"Yeah, as a young guy, operating under his real name. Michael James Dragas, I think it was."

242

Dan nodded.

"That's right. Everything on the up and up back then. Then, one day, a guy welched on a bet. Guy named Oscar Dickworthy. It wasn't even that big a bet. Five hundred bucks! Again and again, Jimmie asked him to pay. And the guy had the means—an architecture student, but he paid nothing. Then one day, Jimmie came to his apartment and begged him for a final time to pay. The guy said he didn't have the money. You know what Jimmie did? He took a butcher's cleaver and chopped off the pinky of Dickworthy's left hand."

I winced at the image.

"Yeah. Then, he sautéed it in olive oil in a frying fan right there in front of him. Then, he made the guy eat it. Knuckles, fingernail, and all. Dickworthy paid him."

"He did?"

Dan nodded vigorously.

"Paid him that very afternoon."

It took me a moment to process this.

"You believe that?"

"How do you think he got his name? Jimmie Flambeau. That's what he fed Dickworthy: fingers flambeau."

"Come on!"

Dan pursed his lips, and his face took on a sage expression.

"I was driving down Lee Highway three or four years ago. I saw a homeless guy in front of the Safeway with a bonkers expression on his face and a missing little finger. Could have been Oscar Dickworthy."

He pushed away from the table with the expression of a man who'd laid down the winning hand.

"I gave him a twenty and kept going."

In the final analysis, it didn't matter if this outrageous tale was true. What mattered was that people like Irish Dan believed it.

Then, I turned it over again in my head.

No, what mattered was that people like Irish Dan *acted* like they believed it.

"Okay. Can you tell him I'm looking for him?"

"If that's what you want. I know he likes doing business with you."

"I want to make sure it stays that way."

I got up and shook his hand.

"See ya, Dan."

I did not count gambling among my vices. I still had all my fingers and I wanted to keep it like that. It also crossed my mind that Heather would disapprove of me getting mixed up with Jimmie Flambeau, but maybe she'd appreciate my willingness to risk my own neck for her. Either way, I figured I had to do whatever it would take to get our desired results.

***

I was expecting a visit from Felipe within a few days. Instead, I got a call from Jimmie. The phone began ringing just as I walked in the door to start the day. Marie smirked and covered the mouthpiece with her hand.

"A Mr. Flambeau?"

"I'll take it in my office."

I shut the door and dropped into the leather chair behind my desk.

"I understand you're looking for me?"

"Yup."

"Business?"

"Yes. Something a little out of the ordinary."

"I figured."

"Can we talk about it?

"Sure. You still got that boat on F Dock?"

Jimmie knew everything about everybody, and he liked to make sure you knew it.

"Yes."

"Can you be there in twenty minutes?"

"Sure."

***

Another thing about Jimmie was that he didn't mind being seen in public. He just didn't like being overheard. I wasn't crazy about being seen with him, but I didn't have much choice.

It took me all of the allotted twenty minutes to get to the marina. Sailboats under auxiliary power made their way to and from the channel and birders and fishermen prowled the green space adjacent to the docks. On the far side of the parking lot, kids and counselors from the sailing camp created a summertime ruckus. The marina was a loud, colorful, and happy place and I picked up on the tangible sense of good cheer.

I pulled into one of the slots reserved for slip holders and before I could exit my car, Jimmie's blue Corvette pulled in beside me. He was driving. No sign of Felipe.

Jimmie was wearing white duck trousers, a blue silk shirt, open to the third button, and a stylish pair of dark glasses. He smiled and offered a friendly handshake. Jimmie was said to be a dour man, but he was also known to maintain friendships with dozens of people. His friendship with Irish Dan Crowley lent Jimmie credibility, and while I didn't feel at ease in his presence, I understood that he operated according to a code of conduct, and if that was acceptable to Irish Dan, it was good enough for me.

I used my marina fob to open the security gate and led Jimmie down the gangplank to the dock. The marina accommodates sailboats only and we walked between two rows of single-hulled day-sailers, most of which had seen better days. Toward the end of the dock on the starboard side lay the *Southern Patriot*, a nineteen-foot sloop that had been carefully maintained until I got it.

We stepped aboard. Most of the updates and improvements in the able little craft had been made by a casual sailor named Jake Carter who had used the boat as his fortress of solitude. From him, it had passed to an old lacrosse connection who had given it to me in lieu of fees.

I had sailed it exactly once since that day and that had been the most consequential day of my life. Time had passed quickly since then and I hadn't found the peace or distance to fully weigh the justice or injustice of my vigilante act. I should have taken that week away on the Massachusetts coast to get my head right. All I could do now was put one foot in front of the other until I got to the end of the road.

I unlocked the cabin, slid open the hatch and took out a pair of sun-faded cushions from the cabin. I placed one on each of the fiberglass banquettes inside the narrow cockpit. Jimmie chose the side that put the sun behind him. The fiberglass on my side was hot to the touch and I sat with my hands folded between my knees until my shadow allowed it to cool.

"Hey, you got this boat from that client of yours, didn't you?"

He showed a thin smile.

"The one who passed?"

Oddly, his effort to goad me allowed me to relax a little.

"Halftrack Racker disappeared, Jimmie. Nobody says he passed."

"I see."

He paused and searched my face and then nodded agreeably.

"Just so you know, it doesn't matter to me."

"Sure."

DP had told me the same thing. But what was quietly reassuring, coming from my friend and collaborator, was deeply unsettling when it came from the mouth of the county's leading criminal.

He was right. *Southern Patriot* had come to me through an ugly client transaction I was trying hard to forget. Jimmie wasn't telling me that he didn't care what had happened. He was telling me that he knew. That's why he wanted to meet here, to squeeze me a little, and now he had set the tone for that.

"Now, what can I do for you?"

"First of all, thanks for coming."

"No problem. You did me a favor."

"It wasn't a big favor."

"It was to me. I owe you one. I told you that."

"Nick Grimes. He paid?"

"Oh yeah, he paid."

I wondered if he knew that Nick Grimes was dead . . . or if he cared. The answer to the first question was almost certainly yes, but I didn't know what to think about the second.

"Any trouble?"

"Nope. Not when I told him what I knew from you about the girlfriend in Delaware."

He suppressed a chuckle. I guessed that this explained Grimes's chilliness when I'd met him at Saigon Breeze.

"Hey, what about you?"

I nodded and glanced beyond the docks to where the Washington Monument loomed above DC's low, marble skyline.

"It's not easy to talk about. I've got a client who's being blackmailed."

He mused for a moment, no more troubled than if I'd asked him to name the capitol of Virginia.

"That ought to be something you can handle without my help."

"I'm glad you think so and I hope that everyone in Arlington County thinks so too, but it's not the kind of thing you can fix with a lawsuit. The truth is, I'm a little out of my depth on this one."

He folded his hands.

"Tell me about the problem."

I nodded.

"The problem is that my client is being blackmailed with something that can be easily duplicated. I've got a deal in place to get it back. How can I be sure I'm getting all the copies?"

"Copies?"

"It's video."

"Have you seen the video?"

"No."

He seemed disappointed in me.

"Then how do you know it's compromising? Or that it's worth what this person says it is?"

"The client told me."

"You trust the client?"

"And I've got a guy who's seen the goods. She's got it on a flash drive."

"Flash drive?"

I described the model Bobbitt used.

He nodded.

"Who's the victim?"

"I'm sorry Jimmie, I'm going to have to hold that back, for now."

That didn't seem to trouble him at all. He nodded and studied the cirrus clouds drifting down the river.

"There's only one way to do it, only one way to be sure. You have to frighten this person and make sure the scare sticks."

There was a time that would have worried me, but I was well past that.

"That's what I figured. That's why I asked to see you."

He nodded agreeably.

"We'll pay this person a visit. That's all."

I suppose I had expected that. There really wasn't any other solution as I saw it and I was encouraged that he wasn't suggesting having Felipe, his ham-handed minion, handle it.

"I don't think it'll take much," I said. "Just a little firm but delicate persuasion."

"Yeah, that's how I see it. We'll have to find the right time and place. Where does this person live?"

"Aldie. She lives alone. It's a quiet place."

"Aldie. Yeah, I know Aldie. Quiet little crossroad town out in the country."

"That's it. She owns the Major Pelham, and she lives in the carriage house out back."

"An ideal set up."

"I think so. The inn is down a side road just past the old mill."

"Perfect!" he said. "It'll take longer to get there than it will to complete our business."

"Shall I set up an appointment?"

"No."

He shook his head casually.

"You pick a time when she'll be home. We'll just show up for a friendly talk. I'll bring Felipe."

"No, I don't want to go in that direction."

He looked at me curiously.

"Felipe gets results. With Felipe, you don't have to worry about the scare part."

"The price is too high. How about just the two of us? I think you can make her see reason."

He shrugged.

"Hey, suit yourself, but my reputation is on the line. You need to understand that."

"I'm sure you'll think of something."

"When do you want to do this?"

"The sooner the better for me."

He thought a minute as he smoothed his dark, thick hair.

"How about tomorrow?"

"Tomorrow works. She's not an early riser. I'll give you the address."

I pulled out a pocket notebook, jotted down the address, tore out the page and handed it to him. He read it out loud several times.

"Good."

Having memorized the address, he tore up the paper and threw the shreds overboard.

"Now, who's the victim?"

I hesitated.

Jimmie would let a lot of things slide, but it wasn't hard to know when he was in earnest. His face hardened, and for a moment I felt at physical risk.

"I need to know," he said. "That's my price."

I didn't hesitate.

"It's Judge Ann Gabriel."

"Easy Ann," he said.

He nodded sagely.

"That's what I figured."

Chapter Twenty-One

Facing The Music

The next morning was hot and humid; hot as blazes, as my mother used to say; hotter than any day we ever experienced on the Massachusetts coast. Heading west away from town and against traffic, it took close to an hour to drive out to Loudoun County, a fast-growing suburb that fought hard to maintain its pockets of quaintness. One of these was the village of Aldie.

As prearranged, I met Jimmie in a Safeway parking lot in nearby Middleburg. I'd been waiting for ten minutes when Felipe pulled up next to me in a new Mercedes. Jimmie, looking casual and relaxed in a blue blazer and gray linen pants, hopped out. After a few terse instructions to Felipe, he got in my car and we drove together to Aldie, where the John Singleton Mosby Highway narrows to two lanes at a gap in the mountains. We found the inn down a poorly paved road just past the old mill.

Everything about the inn conveyed an antebellum authenticity. It occupied a rambling country house of pockmarked, gray brick with green shutters, three chimneys and a slate roof featuring seven gables, all draped with a blanket of English ivy. The parking lot and walkways were composed of gravel and the wooden sign featured a faded portrait of a young Confederate officer on horseback, sword raised dramatically. I recalled learning on my prior visit that the inn had been a well-established way station for weary travelers for years before The Civil War. It was certainly something different now.

The carriage house out back would have been a stable in the days when the blue and gray cavalry fought for control of the mountain gap. I parked out of sight under a grove of trees and turned off the engine. Jimmie sat for a moment, tapping his nose with his index finger.

There was only one car in the lot, a red SUV that matched the description of the vehicle that had picked up Tarry Justice from Bomba's on New Year's Day. Jimmie noted it without any apparent recognition.

"Why don't you take a lap? Make sure she's alone."

It was the first thing he said since getting into my car.

I walked up to a long breezeway, hung with trappings of the hunt—a bugle, a riding helmet, an English saddle, a girth, a bridle, and a pair of Wellington boots. It connected the inn to the single floor carriage house. DP had provided me with its layout: a spacious living room off the breezeway that opened onto three rooms spread across the back, a single bedroom, a kitchen, and a bath.

Through a window, I spotted Bobbitt baking something in the kitchen. I quickly ascertained that there was no one else in the house. I reported this to Jimmie when I got back to my car.

He digested this information, then nodded his head.

"Okay, let's go."

"What a minute."

I touched his arm.

"What's the plan?"

He shook my hand off and glared at me.

"The plan is to get the rest of the flash drives."

"If any."

"Oh, she's got at least one. You can be sure of that."

He got out of the car and moved briskly toward the carriage house, a compact ball of energy and decisive movement. Without the slightest hesitation, he stepped into the breezeway and knocked politely on the glass panel of the door. He gestured toward me with a flick of his stubby fingers.

"Get out of sight."

I stepped down, but to a spot where I could see what was happening.

He knocked again, louder, and we heard an impatient voice from inside.

"Coming, coming."

A hand pushed the curtain aside.

"Mrs. Justice?"

Jimmie gave her a smile and a courtly bow and said something else, but so quietly that I couldn't hear him. Neither could Bobbitt. I heard the bolt turn and she pulled the door open a crack. In a motion almost too quick to follow, Jimmie used the heels of both hands to force the door open, knocking Bobbitt back into the living room, where she stumbled against a baby grand piano and fell into a sitting position on the piano bench.

I followed him in. The spacious room was furnished in Victorian style and period antiques. Jimmie quickly shut and bolted the door and gestured for me to pull the curtains across the windows.

"Who are you?"

Bobbitt was angry, but not cowed, at least until she noticed me.

"You? What are you doing here?"

It was a question I was already asking myself. I had expected to be the brake on Jimmie Flambeau, the voice of reason, but I saw now that there was no room for that. Jimmie's face was alive with an intense and terrifying fervor.

He pointed a finger at her.

"You've got something I want."

Her eyes returned to Jimmie and widened.

"You can have it. Anything."

"You know who I am?"

She picked up a cushion from an adjacent chair and hugged it to her like a shield, shaking her head.

"I'm Jimmie Flambeau."

The name meant nothing to her, and this angered Jimmie.

With a minimalist movement worthy of a magician, he took something from his jacket pocket and held it up. I knew what it was before he flicked the button that released the blade. Bobbitt only recognized it a second later: a heavy, six-inch switchblade.

Jimmie turned it so that the light played on the blade. He spoke gently but forcefully, his voice a diabolical purr.

"I want the flash drives."

"What flash drives?"

"The ones his man came for; the ones you still have."

She looked at me, processing the demand.

"I don't have any more flash drives. His man . . ."

"Oh, but you do."

Jimmie took a step toward her.

"And you're going to give them to me right now or I'm going to hurt you."

Her eyes widened and began to dart.

Jimmie gave her time, letting the terror settle in.

"I don't."

She nodded at me.

"He knows that."

"Break her fingers, Joth."

I did not comprehend exactly what he meant, but the threat was not lost on Bobbitt. She shrank back against the piano.

Jimmie grabbed her left wrist, forced her hand down on the keys with a bang of discordant notes and held it there, the fingers spread across the white keys.

"I'm going to ask you once more."

"No!"

"Where are they?"

"I don't have any more."

His wolfish face narrowed as he assessed her answer.

"Break 'em, Joth!"

When I hesitated, Jimmie grabbed my hand, and with a strength that astonished me, pulled it onto the keyboard cover.

"Smash 'em, Joth!"

"No, no!" Bobbitt said.

She struggled to pull her hand away from his iron grip, but to no avail. As she tried to curl her hand into a ball, he nicked the inside of her wrist with the point of the knife and her hand sprung open. In an instant, his hand grabbed mine and he slammed the keyboard cover down with unrestrained violence on the extended fingers of Bobbitt's left hand. The sound of her fingers fracturing sickened me. She crumpled to the floor, whimpering, holding her damaged hand, and curled into a ball. I saw that the fingers of her left hand had been horribly shattered.

Jimmie stood over her.

"Where is it?"

"I don't know."

She was shrieking in pain.

Her first answer was that she didn't have any, and now she wasn't sure.

Jimmie heard the difference.

"Break her other hand, Joth!"

I stood paralyzed. I had no conception of his capacity for violence.

Bobbitt struggled to her knees and wrapped her arms around Jimmie's legs, hugging them to her.

"No, no, I'll give it to you."

"Just one?"

"There's only one."

"Where is it?"

"Under the bench. The piano bench."

Jimmie nodded to me. I reached beneath the bench and felt around. There was a small shelf built into a recess and I felt the cool metal of a flash drive. I groped around long enough to be sure there were no others. Then, I handed it to Jimmie. He held it up.

"Is this the only one?"

"Yes."

She sobbed.

He looked at her carefully, then slipped the flash drive into his jacket pocket. He displayed the knife again. With his free hand, he took her chin in his hand.

"If another one ever turns up—if it ever turns up— I'm going to come here again."

He showed her the blade.

"I'm going to cut off your little finger. I'm going to sauté it in olive oil right in front of your eyes. And I'm gonna make you eat it. Knuckles, fingernail, and all. You understand?"

"Yes."

She was moaning by now, more broken than terrified.

Jimmie glanced at me to see if my face gave anything away. I'm sure it did.

"Alright then. What happened to your fingers?"

"I don't know," she said.

Bobbitt was thoroughly addled and confused.

"You play the piano, Mrs. Justice?"

She nodded, then shook her head, her eyes clamped shut, unable to speak or comprehend the question.

"If anybody asks, you were playing the piano. The cat got up on the keyboard cover and it came down on your fingers."

"I don't have a cat," she said.

He leaned toward her and glared menacingly.

"Get one."

Jimmie straightened up and put a business card on the piano bench. Glancing at it, I saw the name and address of an orthopedic surgeon.

"Five minutes after we leave, a black Mercedes Benz is going to pull up. A man will be driving. He'll take you to this doctor. He'll see you right away. He'll give you some medicine and he'll fix your fingers. The bill will come to me. And that's the end of our business . . . unless I hear of any other videos."

She nodded.

"Do we understand each other?"

She nodded again. Jimmie gestured toward me, but before he turned in my direction, he had one more thing to add.

"And Mrs. Justice, you can keep making those horrible little home movies of your guests if you want. But you clear each one with me first. Understood?"

She nodded.

"Good. We can do a pretty good business together."

Outside in the parking lot, I was shaken and exhausted. Jimmie looked and sounded as fresh as a daisy.

"Do you mind driving me back to Arlington?"

"But you've got your own car."

"Felipe's going to pick up the lady."

I wanted to be as far away from Jimmie Flambeau as possible, but there didn't seem to be any choice. He waited for me to open the passenger door for him. When I ignored him, he laughed and got in.

We had settled in for the long ride back when Jimmie sighed and shook his head.

"That was hard, but she isn't exactly Saint Teresa."

I assumed he meant Mother Teresa, but he was right. Bobbitt was an extortionist who probably murdered her husband, but she was still a human being. I wondered how good a pianist she had been, because no matter how skilled the orthopedist was, she wasn't going to be playing much piano in the future.

I shook my head. I now understood the secret of Jimmie's power. He was a man with an invincible will, and he was not to be distracted by the cost of collateral damage. I noticed how artfully he had coopted Bobbitt's extortion racket into his expanding enterprise. And I wondered if Bobbitt would do business with him. Something told me she would. Over time, she'd overlook her injury, knowing that Jimmie would keep her safe.

We were more than halfway back before I consolidated my thoughts enough to focus on my original purpose in making this trip.

"I guess you can give me that flash drive now."

"No, I think I'll hang on to it."

I wasn't surprised, only angry at myself for not anticipating this complication.

"That wasn't the understanding, Jimmie."

"We didn't have an understanding except we were going to get it back from her. Which we did."

I didn't speak as I struggled to control my temper. After a few miles, Jimmie filled the vacuum.

"I'll tell you what," he said. "I'll give it back to you, but I want you to do a little legal work or me."

I snuck a wary glance at him.

"What kind of legal work?"

"Legitimate business work. Collections."

"You know gambling debts aren't enforceable in Virginia."

He shrugged.

"It's a defense yes, but only if the debtor raises it. Usually, they'll just settle rather than fight it out. You know, most of my work is entirely legitimate. I own some buildings, so I got to collect rent. And I got contracts to enforce. You know, Felipe, the threats, that's no way to do business."

"You want me to sue these people for you?"

"If necessary. But let's face it, sometimes, a strongly worded demand letter can be just as good. Maybe you get a debt reduced to a promissory note. We could enforce that."

He glanced at me again, smiling.

"You've got a law degree. That's worth a whole lot of muscle."

"I need to think about it."

"Well, you think about it. I'll hang on to the flash drive until you make up your mind."

We were almost back to Arlington. I knew I couldn't afford to let him out of the car with the flash drive.

"What's it pay?"

He shrugged.

"How's this sound: I'll put you on a non-refundable retainer. Let's say $2,000 a month. In cash. Not bad for part-time work."

I was good enough at math to know that this kind of cash would put me in a different tax bracket.

"And I'm just doing collections?"

"Well, whatever comes up. But legitimate legal work, yeah."

I was silent for longer than Jimmie expected.

"I'll tell you what else I'll do," he said. "That thing with Frank Racker, the guy who disappeared? I'll put it out that I'm the one who knows about what happened to him and that it's got nothing to do with you."

"Put it out with who?"

I glanced at him and saw him shrug again.

"Whoever's asking. That cute prosecutor's office for one thing."

My initial reaction was that he'd be taking a big risk, but then I remembered Dan Crowley's story about Oscar Dickworthy. Creating the impression that Jimmie Flambeau was behind a man's unexplained disappearance might be the kind of rumor that would be good for his business.

I didn't give him a chance to change his mind.

"Okay, Jimmie. I think we can work something out along those lines. If I get the flash drive."

We were back in Arlington now, coming up Route 66 toward the District.

"Where am I taking you?"

He pointed out the windshield.

"Turn right here."

After two or three more turns, we came out onto the service road that circled the Marine Corps Memorial and the grassy expanse surrounding it.

"Pull over right there."

I followed his directions and parked where the neatly trimmed grass fell away toward the river and the Lincoln

Memorial on the other side. Jimmie got out of the car and stretched. The heat had broken, leaving a warm and lovely late afternoon. He took his sunglasses off and tilted his face toward the sun.

"This is one of my favorite places," he said.

He slowly turned to admire the famous bronze statue: six American marines planting the stars and stripes atop Mount Suribachi during the battle of Iwo Jima.

"Heroes, these men were. Some of them even gave their lives."

He sighed and shook his head.

"It's chaos that brings peace, you know that Joth? That's what this statue stands for. The sacrifices that must be made for peace and good order."

"Did you serve in the military, Jimmie?"

I asked, even though I already knew the answer. He missed the barb entirely.

"Me?"

He smirked and shook his head.

"No, not me. We've all got different roles to play."

He leaned back against the car, lifting his face to the sun again.

"What are we doing?" I asked.

"Enjoying the day."

After a few minutes, he put his sunglasses back on.

"Okay, let's go."

"Where?"

"You can drop me at Irish Dan's. I know you know where that is."

Ten minutes later, I pulled into a tow-away zone in front of Riding Time. Jimmie shook my hand as he reached into his jacket pocket.

"I'm looking forward to working with you, Joth. This will be a good move for both of us."

He handed me the flash drive, nodded, and got out of the car. I watched him go in and drove hurriedly away.

With Jimmie out of the car, I felt like I could breathe again. I cut through Reagan National Airport to get back to the marina, where I parked outside F Dock. It was a windless afternoon, a day for power boaters on the Potomac. The sailboats were becalmed at their slips and the marina was empty.

I opened the trunk of my car and took out my old Super Light 2, a lacrosse stick with an aluminum shaft and a green, fiberglass head. I hadn't used it since my post-college days, running midfield with the Alexandria club, but it had been a reliable tool for a long time.

I tossed the flash drive Jimmie had given me into the air and snatched it with a flick of my wrists. It was a good feeling. Anything held in the mesh pocket of my stick felt as secure as it would be in a safe. But I had a destiny in mind that was more secure than that.

I cradled the flash drive in the pocket as I made my way across the lot. As I reached the boatyard, I stepped up my speed, dodging dry docked hulls and boat trailers like so many flatfooted midfielders. It was a comforting, once-familiar sensation and I felt quick and light on my feet. I spun and feinted my way to the fringe of woods along the eastern edge of the island, where I found a gap in the trees. Stepping forward, I looked across the flat, slow-moving river toward the distant Maryland shore. I spun the stick once and cranked the old sidearm shot. The flash drive scaled across the channel. It hit and skipped seven times over the wavelets before sinking with a tiny, final splash.

I'd been through an emotionally draining day. I had witnessed, and perhaps participated in an act of physical terrorism, but I'd completed the task. I'd put an end to a career-threatening plot against the only woman who had ever mattered to me. The horror of the tactics used would stick with me, but knowing Bobbitt's sins, I knew the guilt would melt away gradually, like the snow does every March.

Heather would never know about the danger she faced, or what I'd done to end it, but I'd never forget. Plus, Jimmie had promised to make my Track problem go away. I didn't know how he'd do it, but I knew he could.

For the moment, I was exhilarated.

Chapter Twenty-Two

No Way Out

Instead of waiting to regain more of my composure, I called Heather as I was driving home.

"That thing we talked about? That you wanted me to get?"

I paused to tamp down my elation.

"We got it, Heather. DP and me."

I heard her inhale.

"You sure?"

"I'm sure."

"How much?"

"Not a dime. The problem is over."

"Thanks."

I heard her breath again.

"What are you going to do with it?"

"I've already destroyed it. Didn't even look at it."

"So, the person doesn't have to worry about it any-more?"

"Nope, that's all taken care of."

I knew I'd have to pay a price in the form of a period of servitude to Jimmie Flambeau, but I could find a way out of that arrangement if it took me too close to any ethical or legal lines.

"Send me your bill. DP's too. I'll see that they get paid right away."

"Sure."

"And Joth. I hope we won't talk about this again. I hope nobody will."

"Sure. I'll forget it ever happened. DP, too."

"Thanks, Joth. I owe you."

"No. Don't worry about."

"We'll go on like before."

"Just like before."

I didn't know how much Heather knew about what was on that video or how much she now assumed I knew. I hadn't been hired to find out, and she hadn't asked me. She was pulling the curtain over that episode as best she could.

I knew that things would never be quite the same between us again. But maybe, just maybe, they could be better.

***

Two mornings later, Marie announced a pair of un-expected visitors. One was Detective Anderson, the brutish cop, who on a June trip to my office had arrogantly suggested I knew something about the disappearance of Frank Racker.

Instead of Detective McCarthy, his partner on that visit, he was paired with a uniformed officer, named Christine Kelleher. She was a full-bodied woman with compelling blue eyes and a chipper personality that exuded supreme self-confidence. I'd also met her before when she was moonlighting as an errand girl for Jimmie Flambeau. We introduced ourselves as if strangers.

She was doing the talking today.

"Can we have a few minutes of your time, Mr. Proctor?"

I shot a glance at Anderson. He was subdued and avoided eye contact. I was curious, but by no means anxious.

"Sure, why not? Come on in."

I offered them the captain's chairs across from my desk.

Kelleher's expression was amiable, but she got right to the point.

"I think you know that Detective Anderson here has been spearheading a task force looking into the disappearance of Frank 'Halftrack' Racker in late May."

"Yes, he and I have talked about that."

"Well, we've come upon some new information we're trying to tie down. Are you acquainted with a man who calls himself Jimmie Flambeau?"

"Sure. I know him."

"Friends?"

"No, we're not friends."

"Do you work for him?"

I knew she was speaking in her professional capacity, but also as an emissary of Flambeau, and that this Kabuki theater was both a message and a test.

"He's a businessman. I'll do work for any businessman who finds himself in trouble and can pay for it."

She nodded as she processed the answer.

"Mr. Flambeau employs a man named Felipe Pasquale. Do you know him?"

"We've met."

"There's reason to believe that Pasquale was the last person to see Racker before he disappeared."

So, that was Jimmie's play. I took a breath.

"When was that?"

She conspicuously consulted her notebook.

"That would have been on May 25th."

May 25th was the day after my last contact with Racker. The day after I'd dumped his lifeless body into the Potomac.

"I see. What's that got to do with me?"

"We know you represented Racker until at least late May. We wondered if you'd seen the two of them together."

I thought about this for a long moment. Jimmie was throwing his top henchman overboard and he was giving me the chance to cut the line.

"Do you know where they were seen together?"

"Yes, our information shows that they had lunch at the Fish Market on King Street in Old Town."

I nodded. I was ready to bet Jimmie had given her the receipt.

"I'd have to check my calendar, but I don't think I was in Old Town that day and I know I haven't eaten at the Fish Market since last winter."

"I see. So, you didn't see them together at or around that date?"

"No, I'm sure I didn't."

"Did you ever hear Racker mention Pasquale?"

Kelleher was giving me a free shot at Felipe. I didn't particularly object to what Jimmie was doing, but I wasn't going to help.

"No, he never did, not that I can remember."

She glanced at Anderson who had nothing to add. When she stood up, so did the detective. She handed me a business card.

"If you think of anything that might help us, could you give us a call?'

"Of course."

***

I escorted them out to the lobby, where we exchanged handshakes and professional pleasantries. As I watched them cross the parking lot toward Courthouse Road, I wondered if Felipe knew that his boss was selling him out. He wasn't going to be happy when he found out.

"What did they want?"

It was DP, leaning on the door frame of the conference room. I turned and grinned at him.

"Where have you been hiding?"

"I'm back in business and I'm busy."

He nodded toward the parking lot.

"What about those two?"

"Looks like the heat's off on Racker's disappearance."

I sighed. Voicing this truth allowed the tension to dissipate.

"They're on to someone else now."

"They came here to tell you that?"

"No, they came following up on their new lead."

"And who's the new scapegoat?"

"Felipe Pasquale."

DP studied me carefully. He knew Pasquale and he knew who he worked for.

"You want to tell me about it?"

"Sure, come on in."

***

Once inside my office, DP shut the door and dropped heavily into one of the client chairs, but I was still giddy and didn't pick up on his mood.

"I've done a lot since I saw you last," I said.

"Have you?"

"You were right. Bobbitt was holding onto a last flash drive."

"And you got it back?"

"Yeah."

"How'd you do that?"

"I got Jimmie Flambeau to help a little bit."

DP got out of his chair and walked impulsively toward the window, where he stood with his hands on his hips, looking out on Wilson Boulevard.

"And what was his price?"

"He didn't have a price."

He pivoted and looked at me like I was an idiot. I felt a chill run down my spine.

"He owed me a favor."

"And?"

"And, I said I'd do a little legal work for him. You know, legit stuff."

He sat down in the chair again and looked distractedly at the print on the wall above the credenza: the House of the Seven Gables.

"So that was his price for helping you get the flash drive back?"

"He told me he'd take the heat off me on Racker."

"Which he did by throwing Felipe to the wolves?"

"Looks like it."

"Who's going to take Felipe's role in his organization?"

DP was putting the pieces together in a way I had not, or at least had not wanted to. I saw that I had been flailing, throwing up logical responses, trying to slow the steady march of facts that I did not want to acknowledge.

"It'll be different." I said. "I'm just going to enforce his contractual rights."

I said the right thing but was no longer sure I believed it.

"Yeah? And who's going to do Felipe's job?"

"He's changing his business model."

"Yeah."

DP held out his hand.

"Let's see the flash dive."

"I don't have it."

"Where is it?"

"I threw it in the river."

"You threw it in the river."

He repeated it with a shake of his head.

"I don't suppose you looked to see what was on it first?"

"No. Jimmie scared the hell out of Bobbitt. I'm sure she gave him what she had."

"So, she gave it to Jimmie?"

"Yeah."

His crossed a leg over his knee.

"How did you get it?"

I hesitated to relate Jimmie's abuse of Bobbitt.

"He got her to admit that she'd had one copy hidden away."

"Where was that?"

"On a little shelf under the seat of the piano bench."

DP nodded

"I didn't look there."

I folded my arms and looked at him smugly.

"Well, I'm the one who dug it out."

"Congratulations. And then you gave it to Jimmie?"

"Yeah, but he gave it back to me."

"Tell me about that."

"It was on the drive back. We argued about it a little. He said he'd give it to me if I agreed to do legal work for him every once in a while. He offered me a good rate."

"And you said yes?"

He'd already thought this through more than I had. But that was alright with me. He was plowing ahead like a good prosecutor, not giving me time to think through my answers.

"That's right," I said. "I agreed."

"And then he gave you the flash drive?"

"Yeah."

"Where was it?"

"What do you mean 'where was it?' "

"Where did he put it after you gave it to him?"

"In his jacket pocket."

"Which jacket pocket?"

"The pocket in the side of his jacket."

"Which side. Right or left?"

I thought back.

"It was his right pocket."

"Are you sure?"

I didn't answer. Things had happened so quickly that my memory of the event was hazy and unclear.

"Is that the same pocket he took it out of?"

I stared at DP as I processed the implication of his question.

"Of course, it was."

He looked at me probingly.

"But you don't know, do you?"

When I didn't answer, he shook his head sadly.

"He palmed it."

"What do you mean?"

"He took a flash drive out of his pocket and gave it to you. How do you know it's the same one he got from Bobbitt?"

I tried to think back. I could remember what the one he'd given to me in the car looked like, but I couldn't recall the one I'd taken from under the bench.

"They were the same," I said. "A plastic piece with a U-shaped metal loop that swings down to protect the connector."

"What color was the plastic?"

I could envision the one that I whipped into the river.

"The one I threw into the river was purple."

"And the one you found under the piano bench?"

I hadn't noticed or couldn't remember. My recollection of that visit was stuck on the image of Bobbitt's mangled fingers, and DP read the truth on my face.

"He was one step ahead of you, Joth. Jimmie knew you were going there to get a flash drive, so he had a blank one in his pocket."

"I don't believe it."

"And now you can't even check. He's still got it; you can be sure of it. You're going to have to get it back from him. Heather won't be safe until you do."

I knew that this was true. The whole sordid enterprise was concocted to get blackmail material out of the hands of someone who might be willing to use it. If DP was right, it was now in the hands of someone who was certainly willing to use it.

Before I could speak, the intercom buzzed.

"A Mr. Flambeau for you? He says he's a client."

DP's face collapsed into an expression of horror and regret. In a flash, I saw that I was on the road to becoming a corrupt lawyer and that this is how it happens—not as a result of intelligent choices, but through the incremental tug of circumstances.

I asked DP to leave and took the call.

Coming Soon!

FRIEND OF THE DEVIL
BOOK 4
A JOTH PROCTOR FIXER MYSTERY
BY
JAMES V. IRVING

After gambler and loan shark Jimmie Flambeau leverages Joth into an uncomfortable professional relationship, Joth and private detective DP Tran develop a high risk plan to deliver Heather from impending disaster. As nerves are frayed and lines crossed, Joth stumbles on to a clue to a decades old mystery – and then ghosts from his past intrude.

For more information
visit: www.SpeakingVolumes.us

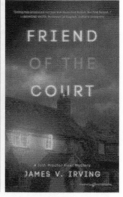

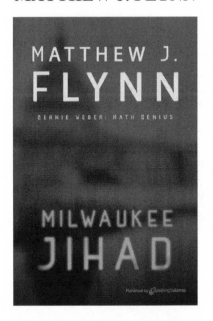